BLUE RIDGE DANGER

CAROLYN LAROCHE

HOT TREE PUBLISHING

BLUE RIDGE DANGER

MARSHALL BROTHERS
BOOK 4

CAROLYN LAROCHE

HOT TREE PUBLISHING

For information, contact the publisher, Hot Tree Publishing.

WWW.HOTTREEPUBLISHING.COM

EDITING: HOT TREE EDITING

COVER DESIGNER: BOOKSSMITH DESIGN

E-BOOK ISBN: 978-1-923252-27-1

PAPERBACK ISBN: 978-1-923252-28-8

For Carlos,
You finally made it into a book!

PROLOGUE

"Just let the hostages go and come out with your hands up!" Carter Marshall did his best to sound authoritative yet understanding, but after two hours of "negotiating" with an armed man threatening to kill at least half a dozen people and who also refused to respond to any attempts at conversation, he was pretty sure he sounded more impatient than anything. Droplets of perspiration dotted his forehead despite the cool evening temperatures. His muscles ached from the adrenaline that had flooded them for hours, but still, he held his position.

This wasn't his first rodeo with hostage negotiation. He'd done it enough times to know the procedures and always came out on top—saving the hostages and arresting the suspect.

Unfortunately, nothing had been textbook procedure with this guy, and it had really begun to wear Carter down. Desperation to get the man to give in even a little fed the adrenaline that fueled his stubbornness. He *would* end this standoff—come hell or high water. And based on the darkness moving in across the mountains, both hell and high waters were very solid possibilities.

An open window was the only means of reaching out to the perp. A direct line into the house had gone unanswered, as had several of the hostages' cell phones. Unsure if anyone inside could even hear him, Carter continued to speak to the perp in the hopes of eventually getting a response.

The whole thing had become very frustrating, not to mention mentally exhausting. From his position behind a tree with a line of sight to the open window, he considered his options.

The SWAT officers from the state police stood posted all around the old farmhouse, waiting for the command to breach. Officers from Carter's own department also stood at the ready, just waiting for him to say the word.

That command would put a lot of innocent lives in a whole lot more danger of dying, though, so he refrained—despite wanting this whole thing to be over already. Their quiet town would take years to recover from this.

He tried a different tactic. Moving to a closer tree, he called out, "Come on, man! At least let the rest of them go! They have no beef with you, and I'm sure you don't have one with them!"

"You don't know anything about who I got problems with!"

Carter's heart kicked up its pace. Finally!

He called out again. "Just open the door and send the hostages out! Then we can discuss your terms!"

"I don't got any terms! I just want them all off our land! Leave me and my girl alone! That's all I want."

The perp sounded a little bit desperate. Good. That meant he was also getting tired.

"Then send them out to us, and we can get them off your land!"

After a long stretch of silence, the front door to the house opened slowly. Carter held up a hand and said, *"Hold your fire,"* into the mic on his shoulder.

"Fine! Don't shoot! I'm sending them out!"

The perpetrator definitely sounded exhausted. Carter's energy renewed. He hadn't expected the man to cave so quickly.

"No one is going to shoot!" To the officers around him he yelled, "Hold your fire!"

They all watched in silence as four men and two women exited the farmhouse, many of them sobbing and holding on to each other. Medics and officers met them a hundred feet from the porch and ushered them to the ambulances that stood ready down the long drive.

"You have the hostages! Now go away!" the perpetrator yelled. "Those are my terms. Just leave us alone."

"Please don't leave me here with him!" a woman cried. "He's got a gun! I don't want to die!"

Her last words ended on a sob, tugging at Carter's heart. This whole situation needed to end, and it needed to end immediately.

"You know we can't leave, man," Carter shouted back, working hard at containing his frustration. "What do you say we call it a day, and you let the woman go? Then you and I can talk things out."

"Yeah, right! And then you'll have the perfect opportunity to shoot me. I'm not an idiot, despite what my brother thinks!"

Finally, something to work with. "Is that why we're here? Because of your brother?"

"Leave my brother out of this!" A weird mix of defensive annoyance wrapped around his words.

"Hey, man, you brought him up." Carter moved forward, slowly trying to get close enough to see through the window.

"We're here because I love her, but *he* filled her head with a bunch of lies about me. I'm just trying to make her understand that none of it is true!"

By holding her and a bunch of people hostage? This guy was more than a little off.

"Why don't you let me come in and have a talk with her? I've got four brothers—I know how annoying they can be. Always making stuff up and trying to cause me trouble."

He made it to the side of the house. Pressing himself up against it, he leaned forward ever so slightly to peer through a narrow split in the curtains that hung over the open window. A man with his back to the window held a gun against the chest of a woman. Fear had frozen her features in a look Carter would never forget. Tears ran down her face as she begged her captor to let her go. No one else appeared to be left in the house.

"I promise, I don't believe any of it," she whispered. Her body trembled as she reached toward the man, trying to take his hand. "I love you, baby. You know I do."

"Do you really expect me to believe you?" He jabbed the gun against her sternum, causing her to stumble backward and land on a sofa. "You tried to run away when I showed up."

"I was working! We're trying to set up filming here! I wasn't running away. I was trying to direct my crew." She broke down into heavy tears. "I don't even know what you're talking about!"

"Yes. You. Do." He punctuated each word with another jab to her chest. "He filled your head with *lies,* and now you're lying for *him!*"

"Why would I lie for him when I'm with you?" The woman sobbed through her words.

"I've got a clear shot," someone said in Carter's earpiece. *"Just let me end this already."*

"Not yet," someone else replied. *"If he has a gun on her, he'll shoot as he goes down."*

For whatever reason, his earpiece decided to let out a loud screech of interference. Carter cringed, knowing his position had been compromised. The man inside spun around and aimed his gun at the window.

"Run!" Carter yelled to the woman. Without hesitating, she jumped up and fled from the room.

Simultaneously, he called, "*Now!*" into his mic as he fired several shots at the perp.

A burst of gunfire sounded in the house, bullets penetrating the wall he leaned against. One slammed into his thigh, and Carter dropped to his knees, attempting to crawl away. Too late.

All around him, every single armed officer fired at the farmhouse in a hail of projectiles. Two more bullets pierced his body, one in his left shoulder and another penetrating the side of his abdomen, right below the tactical vest he wore. Shots came so fast and from every direction. He had no idea if they were friendly fire or from the perp, just that he was caught in the middle. Panic seized him as the pain increased with every bullet.

The hot lead seared through layer after layer of soft tissue. Pain engulfed him with all the intensity of a lightning strike, taking his breath with it. He gasped, trying to refill his lungs, but instead his mouth filled with the taste of copper.

Blood.

A heart-wrenching sound he could only describe as the wail of death itself emanated through the air as the SWAT officers breached the door and swarmed into the house. Eerie silence followed the agonizing cry. For a full thirty seconds, not a single sound permeated the air except his own gasps for air. The silence became replaced by a ringing in his ears that nearly drowned out the chaos that suddenly ensued all around him.

"We need medics in here *now!*" one of the officers in the house demanded, sounding panicked. "And by now, I mean ten minutes ago!"

Everywhere around him, people ran and barked commands, but no one seemed to notice his injured and bleeding body lying in the grass. Neither his arms nor legs would move as Carter's vision began to darken around the edges. His slowing heart rate told him that if he wasn't found soon, it would be too late.

He tried to call for help, wave a hand, move, *something*, but it felt as though his brain had completely disconnected from the rest of his body. A thick, wet cough spewed blood that trailed along his jaw and down his neck.

Sending up a silent prayer for forgiveness, he allowed himself to succumb to the dark peace moving in. Just as his eyes were about to close, someone grabbed his hand. Their touch was soft but firm. The scent of fresh citrus overtook the air, almost drowning out the smell of blood and death.

"We need help over here!" The woman, whose voice he did not recognize, knelt beside him, feeling for a pulse in his wrist. He'd heard the frantic plea in her words, confirming just how bad things were.

With the last bit of strength he had, Carter opened one eye to see a striking brunette staring down at him. Her green eyes were dark with worry. The way the sun hung low in the sky behind her created a halo effect that bathed her in soft light.

Like an angel.

"You're awake!" She patted his hand, smiling through her obvious concern. "Stay with me, officer. Just hang on. Help is on the way."

"I'm sorry," Carter whispered, squeezing her hand lightly before the darkness took over and her light was gone.

CHAPTER ONE

Inhaling deeply, Carter let the fresh mountain air wash away the stress of the past few weeks. All the back-and-forth with the television network over contracts and such had definitely taken its toll.

When he and his youngest brother, Josh, had first purchased the old, run-down campground, Carter had never expected to be able to live here and run his business full time for another few years or more. It had begun as a "someday, when he retired" project that had turned into reality when life took a complete one-eighty on him over a year ago. His forced retirement from the police department had given him little choice, but what had started out as the worst nightmare of his life had ended up being a huge blessing. Over time, he and Josh had cleaned the place up, erected a new dining hall and dorm, and started the ball rolling on the Blue Ridge Mountains Campground and Survival School.

The agreement with the Hollywood-based television network felt a little bit like a miracle and a little bit like a deal with the devil.

Still, there was no denying that the one thing that had haunted him night and day had also presented him with the opportunity to finally realize his dream.

Carter exhaled, counting to ten the way his therapist had taught him to. He needed to relax and take control of the memories that constantly waited to destroy him.

Josh's old Jeep CJ sat parked in front of the cabin that acted as the office for the facility. Josh had a gift for running things—crunching numbers, seeing the big business picture, and making things come together. Despite his own position as the newest rookie of the Staunton, Virginia, police department, Josh knew a good moneymaking opportunity when he saw one. Lately, he'd been spending a lot more time here. Carter suspected his brother's increased involvement in the facility had a lot to do with Carter's near-death experience. Josh had probably been elected by their other three brothers to keep an eye on him after the dark place Carter had been in not all that long ago.

The sound of an engine straining hard echoed among the trees, breaking him from his reverie. The road up to the campground was steep, narrow, and winding. It took something with a lot of power to make it without taxing the engine too much—or at the very least someone who understood how to downshift.

A cloud of dust preceded the screaming engine and spinning tires. Carter watched as a little red sports car pulled into view.

The windows were tinted far too dark for him to see inside. *Illegal tinting gives probable cause for a search,* his cop brain reminded him.

I am not a cop anymore.

His brain laughed at him. *Once a cop, always a cop.*

Shut up, brain.

Carter walked toward the tiny car that had no place in a rustic campground. Someone was either lost, running from the cops—oops, they'd messed that one up, since Josh was there—or hauling drugs. Again, bad choice of destination.

I told you to shut up, brain. Stop thinking like a cop all the time!

Resting his left hand on his hip where his gun used to sit, he started forward with purpose, ready to respond to any threat. Then Carter stopped moving, forcing himself to relax his stance. There was no threat.

He certainly didn't expect a *threat* to have long tanned legs, a little black dress, and some ridiculously high, strappy black heels.

The curvy brunette who had stepped from the car couldn't have looked more out of place on his mountain. And yet, she acted like she totally belonged there.

Because she did. Somehow, this place welcomed her as though she'd lived here all her life. A little flicker of memory began to form in his mind. He knew her. He knew her in this place, not just through calls and emails.

"Carter Marshall." She stepped closer, her hand outstretched. His name was a statement, not a question. "I'm Rylie Christianson. From the television network."

When he heard her voice, which he'd encountered a dozen times over the phone, all the pieces suddenly came together. She was his angel of mercy as he lay dying in the grass.

The hotshot television producer he'd exchanged calls and emails with for months and the gentle woman who had saved his life were one and the same. How had he not realized it before?

Still, she seemed sorely out of place in the short little dress and stiletto heels. She needed boots and a flannel.

His heart did a little fluttery thing as he imagined her in one of *his* flannels.

Clearing his throat to erase the very unexpected image, Carter studied her from head to toe, an eyebrow raised in question at the outfit she wore. "You can't be serious."

She thrust her hands onto her hips. "What's that supposed to mean?"

He scowled as he motioned to her clothes. "The woman I talked to is looking to film a survival show. You look like you're planning to film *America's Next Top Model*. If that's what you're here for, get back in that fancy little impractical ride of yours and drive right back down the mountain. And try to do it without destroying your transmission."

Rylie returned his scowl and raised him an eye

roll. "Do you always judge a book by its cover, Mr. Marshall?"

She held his stare with a challenge in her own green eyes. Carter slightly relaxed his stance, ignoring the tiny frisson of awareness that ran through him as she stared him down.

Carter inhaled slowly, counting to three. Sometimes he forgot how to act around normal people.

"Yeah, no. Sorry." He took another deep breath as he accepted her hand in his, nearly jerking it back at the little shock of electricity that arced between them. "You just caught me off guard. Most people don't come up here in heels and fancy wheels, you know? We're a trucks and boots kinda operation."

It was a crappy recovery, but it was the best he had to offer. Fortunately, Rylie didn't seem to be put off by it as she shrugged and laughed. "The man's a poet, and he didn't know it."

Carter let go of her hand and shoved his fingers through his hair. "Welcome to the Blue Ridge Mountains Campground and Survival School."

"Thank you so much for offering up your property. We—I—really appreciate it. Finding a new location that worked for the show and hadn't been a violent crime scene was extremely difficult."

Her reference to that day caught him off guard.

"Are you okay?" Rylie gave him an inquisitive once-over, making him even more uncomfortable.

He offered up a small smile. "Yes, sorry. It's been a long day." Carter turned and started walking toward the office. "Follow me, and we'll get things going."

He stopped moving when he felt a hand on his shoulder. "Mr. Marshall?"

Carter turned to look at the woman. She wore a dozen different, clashing emotions on her tanned face, making her green eyes swirl like a hurricane. Never mind the heat and confusion her touch created.

"Are you sure you're okay with this?" she asked, the concern genuine. "I know that was a very hard day for you."

He could tell she chose her words carefully, despite memories that were likely as clear for her as they were for him.

Taking a step back to lose the contact of her touch, Carter swallowed against the onslaught of emotion. "I'm sure. After all, I owe you my life. It's a debt I could never fully repay no matter what I do." Discomfort and shame washed through him at the look of pure sadness on her face. "Let's get you a key and get you settled."

Turning on his heel, he strode to the office and yanked the door open. Much to her credit, Rylie kept pace despite the heels she wore.

"Josh?" he called as he closed the door behind them.

"In here!" his youngest brother replied from the small second room of the cabin that he'd turned into his workspace. In the cabin's previous life, it would have been the bedroom. In the main room, where Carter and Rylie stood, they'd added a counter and a few other amenities needed for running a business.

"This is absolutely perfect." Rylie spun in a slow circle. "I'll set up over there on the counter, if that's okay. Y'all got Wi-Fi up here, or am I going to have to go old-school with dial-up?"

"You won't need this office. There's Wi-Fi in your cabin. And everywhere in the main camp-ground area."

Carter strode into the back room where his brother sat in front of a laptop computer and several stacks of papers. "Stacks" being a stretch, as the piles had been strewn over every bit of the polished wooden surface.

"Hey, Josh, this is—"

She stepped in front of him, hand held out to Josh. "Rylie Christianson. I'm the producer of the new reality show *Survive This*." Her wide, warm smile lit up her entire persona.

"Have we met before?" Josh asked. "You look so familiar to me."

She smiled warmly. "I don't think *you* and I have ever met before."

Josh turned crimson. "Sorry. I could have sworn we have."

Carter held back a chuckle at Rylie's effect on the youngest Marshall. Josh wouldn't have a clue what to do with a woman like her. Or pretty much any woman, for that matter.

As predicted, his shy, number-crunching brother turned bright red. Extending his hand, Josh knocked one of his haphazard stacks of files toward Rylie, showering her in paper.

Josh flushed an even deeper russet that darkened his tanned skin. "I'm so sorry!" He looked like he would die of embarrassment.

Rylie waved it away with a bright smile. "No worries. Nothing to apologize for. You should see my office back at the studio."

His brother now looked like he wanted the floor to open up beneath him and swallow him whole. He grabbed a stack of papers held together by a black binder clip and offered them to Rylie. "This is the contract and the releases I need you to sign before your contestants get here."

She gave him another smile. "Thank you. I'll get this back to you as soon as I'm done."

Carter turned to the woman and motioned back toward the other room. "Let me show you to your cabin, Ms. Christianson."

"Please, call me Rylie." Her warm smile made him want to call her anything she wanted.

What the heck was going on with him? Rylie represented the single most important moment of his life. A living, breathing reminder of his own mortality and a life that no longer existed.

Maybe this was one of those PTSD triggers his therapist had talked about. Something about Florence Nightingale attachment or whatever.

He exhaled slowly. "Come on, Rylie. Let's get you settled."

Glancing back at his brother, Carter winked when Josh mouthed a silent thank-you. Lightly placing a hand at the small of Rylie's back like it was the most normal thing in the world, he directed her out of the office. As they passed a cabinet on the wall, Carter grabbed the key labeled Cabin 6. The cabin directly beside his, which may or may not have been the best idea. Jamie, his therapist, probably wouldn't approve.

As they stepped outside, he eyed her little car. "Do you have bags or equipment or anything?"

Rylie pointed at the back of her car. "My things are in there. My cameraman will be here later today with some cameras and other equipment to get us started. The rest of the crew, equipment, and contestants arrive first thing in the morning the day after tomorrow."

She pulled her key ring from the overly large shoulder bag she carried and popped open the trunk of the vehicle. Carter stepped in front of her, reaching in and lugging out the two large and surprisingly heavy duffel bags crammed into the small space.

"I can do that. I don't travel light." She reached over to grab the bags from him, but Carter evaded her by stepping backward.

"I'm sure you can, but I don't mind."

"Seriously. Your injuries—"

"Are completely healed," Carter grunted as he took another step out of her reach.

Rylie's quick reaction caused her to stumble forward on her ridiculously inappropriate shoes. Carter dropped the bags onto the ground beside him to steady her at the same moment that the woman crashed solidly against his chest. She grabbed at his shirt to steady herself as he wrapped his arms around her waist. They both toppled backward anyway, landing with a thump on a soft moss-covered area.

"Hmpf!" Carter exhaled hard as his lungs compressed from the fall.

Rylie lay on top of him, her face pressed against his chest. After a good ten seconds had passed, she pulled away and gave him a shy little smile. "I've always been good at making a dramatic entrance." She pushed up to a sitting position. "I'm so sorry. Are you hurt?"

Her green eyes held all the compassion and concern she'd showed him that day. Her gentle touch and insistence that someone help him were the two things that had probably saved his life.

A decision he'd been regretting every second since he'd said yes. At the moment, that regret had switched gears to a straight-up "What the hell have I done?" This woman, his literal lifesaver, would be living within arm's reach for the better part of a month, and based on his body's reaction to her extreme proximity, that might be a huge mistake.

"Those shoes are downright dangerous. Don't you have boots or... anything other than those to wear?" he grumbled. Rylie straddling him in that sexy-as-hell dress had him all jumbled up inside.

He needed distance, and he needed it *right then*.

Rolling to the side, he carefully attempted to disengage their bodies. Everything would have been fine, too, if the hem of her too-short dress hadn't gotten caught on the clip holding his knife in place in his pocket. As Carter attempted to jump to his feet, a loud ripping sound filled the space around them. He froze.

Rylie's dress tore clear up her thigh to her waist, completely baring one smooth, tanned thigh and teasing him with the other. The rush of warmth that filled his face rivaled the heat coursing through his veins. He literally prayed that a giant, gaping sinkhole would form right there and swallow him along with his embarrassment.

Taking a deep breath, he dared to look her in the eyes. "I am so sorry, ma'am. Let me know the cost, and I'll pay for it."

The humor he found in her expression was nothing like the anger he'd expected to see. "This ain't my first roll in the leaves, sir. Things happen— clothes rip, earrings get lost. No biggie. It's my fault anyway. I should have just let you be chivalrous or whatever."

Her nonchalance at their predicament, however, only fueled the embarrassment threatening to devour him. "Still, I am really sorry. I'll pay for it—seriously."

Rylie made no attempt to cover her legs as his face continued to flush with heat. "Let's just get separated first, and then we can discuss specifics later."

After finally managing to unhook her dress from his knife clip, Carter stood up and extended a hand to Rylie. Her entire left thigh was still exposed, the skin even more tanned and smooth than first glance had indicated. His heart accelerated and his breath caught.

Carter gulped. No. This was not part of the plan.

She accepted his assistance to get her back on her feet. "Bless your heart, if you don't turn the most adorable shade of red when you're embarrassed."

Rylie smoothed what was left of her dress down, sweeping away bits of leaves and dirt. A piece of a twig stuck out of the side of her head, tangled in her hair. As she kicked off her heels, Carter reached up and pulled the stick from her hair before tossing it to the ground.

"Are you injured anywhere?" he asked.

Rylie nodded. "Only my pride. I'm sorry I

knocked you down. Which one of these little sheds is for me?"

"They're cabins." Carter scowled, his embarrassment switching to annoyance as he pointed at one. "That *cabin* is for you. Your assistant gets the one next to you, and the rest of the crew can have the dormitory." He motioned to a long, low building about five hundred yards away. "There's a small bathroom in your cabin. The dormitory is serviced by a bathhouse located behind it."

Without another word, he strode away. Already completely flustered by the afternoon's events, Carter really needed a hot shower, a beer, and a chance to get the memory of Rylie Christianson pressed against him out of his brain.

CHAPTER TWO

RYLIE SIGHED AS SHE PUSHED OPEN THE DOOR TO the tiny cabin. Carter had no idea who she was. Not really. To him, she was just the woman who had helped him at the shooting. She dropped her bags inside the door and leaned against the wall. The space was basic but impressively clean and neat with a single bed along one wall, a tiny table with a chair on either side, and a lamp set in the middle. The narrow chest of drawers completed the main space. Rylie closed the door and, with a loud groan, dropped face-first onto the faded quilt that covered the bed. After her failed grand entrance, her gut said this would be a rough few weeks.

She might never be able to tell him who she really was after that major flop.

As soon as she had kicked off those stupid heels, Rylie felt more like herself. Her entire body relaxed at once. The successful television producer persona she'd created to impress Carter Marshall had been completely fruitless. He'd been 100 percent unimpressed, particularly after she tackled him to the ground for trying to help with her bags. The outfit and car had been Jack's idea. She never should have listened to him. The man didn't have a clue about how to interact with other humans. His level of social awkwardness was off the charts.

Her host had looked at her with such disdain, it had her hackles up. Grabbing that bag from him had been a knee-jerk reaction that had definitely not ended well.

Not that she hated feeling his hard strength against every inch of her body. There was something about him that just felt like home to her. According to the therapist the network had sent her to, it was some sort of "Clara Barton response" from having saved his life.

She'd laughed it off at first, but now she wondered how much truth there was to that whole lifesaver syndrome concept. Seeing the man in person after so many months, and looking fit and healthy aside from the haunted look deep in his eyes, had done something to her insides that she wasn't exactly proud of.

Carter Marshall had absolutely no idea how that slightly annoyed smolder of his affected women.

Now she had to spend the better part of a month in close proximity to a grumpy man at a worn-out campground if she wanted to make Darcy's dream a reality.

Rylie had done her research. Thanks to the infinite amount of information on the internet, she'd discovered that the cranky, incredibly good-looking man had once been a somewhat awkward, lanky teenager with clear blue eyes and a smile that could stop any girl in their tracks and make them swoon.

Very different from the man with the dark, stormy expression that he had become. Darcy's murder and his own near-death experience had obviously taken their toll.

Memories of that day never quite left her alone. The death of her best friend and the bloodied body of the man who had almost given his own life trying to save that friend had created a sadness in her very soul.

Rylie rose and walked to the tiny bathroom to clean up. Catching sight of herself in the small wall mirror, she sighed. Dirt smears on her face, bits of dried leaves in her hair, and the destroyed dress just added to the horror of the day.

I'll take bad decisions for $1000, Alex.

Rylie stripped out of the awful dress and tossed it into a corner. Even if it weren't destroyed, she'd never have worn that stupid thing again.

"I'm not going to mess this up, Darcy. I promise." Her words held far more conviction than she felt.

Standing in front of the mirror in her bra and panties, Rylie scowled at the makeup she wore. All the hours of internet videos had only taught her that she really hated the stuff.

"Who are you even trying to kid, girl?" she asked her reflection as she pulled her hair up into a messy bun on top of her head. Rylie grabbed the soap off the counter and set about washing the makeup from her face.

A noise outside the tiny bathroom window caught her attention. Turning, she looked straight into the blue eyes of Carter Marshall. Only his eyes weren't exactly looking at hers. In fact, they were looking at every inch of her *except* her eyes.

His gaze rose to meet hers. When he realized he'd been discovered, he snapped out of whatever trance he'd been in. His face turned beet red, and he mouthed something that was probably a curse. It sure wasn't *"Oh my God, I'm so sorry I got caught staring at you in your underwear."*

As he hurried away, the toe of Carter's boot caught a raised tree root, and he stumbled. After a series of not at all graceful moves, he regained his balance and basically ran around the corner of the building.

Rylie laughed. Served him right for peeping in her window anyway. In that brief moment, he'd looked just like that boy she'd first met so many years ago.

From her bag on the narrow bed, her cell phone chimed, indicating a text message coming in. Drying her face with a surprisingly soft and fluffy hand towel, Rylie walked over and pulled out the phone. Her cameraman Jack Benson's number showed up on the screen. Before opening the message, Rylie pulled a long-sleeved top over her head and slipped into a pair of leggings. The cabin air had a chill to it.

She retrieved the phone again and opened the messaging app.

> Jack: You find the place okay?

> Rylie: Yeah. The clothes and car were a dumb idea. This place is RUSTIC.

She dug her boots out of the bag and stepped into them, pulling the laces taut.

> Jack: I bet you looked hot. Like a real television producer.

> Rylie: Knock it off, Jack. What time will you be here?

> Jack: Not until the morning. Something came up.

> Rylie: Your contract starts tonight.

> Jack: Unavoidable. Sorry to leave you alone with the mountain man. I'll get up there as soon as I can.

A whole night on the mountain with the two Marshall brothers didn't seem so awful to her. Far better than being alone in her tiny apartment night after night.

> Rylie: Fine. Actually it's two mountain men. He has a younger brother.

> Jack: I guess you're safe from the bears and mountain lions, then.

> Rylie: I was never worried. I really need to start working up the set, so get up here early.

Jack: I'll be there as early as I can.
Family stuff. You know how it is.

Of all the camera operators at the network, Jack was her least favorite. He was far less skilled at outdoor camera work than some of the other operators, and it was his brother who had killed Darcy, yet he was the one they paired her with.

Maybe Jack thought he could somehow offer reparations for the acts his brother had committed by seeing Darcy's dream through to the end.

Maybe he blamed Carter Marshall and wanted to be sure he knew it by reminding him at every opportunity he got. Honestly, that seemed more like the Jack she knew.

Rylie sighed heavily. Something she'd been doing a lot the past several months.

If only the original cameraman could have done it. Apparently getting held at gunpoint by a crazy murderer was more than he could handle, though, as he'd handed in his resignation the very next day.

Whatever the reason, she was stuck with Jack and his weird humor and unpredictable personality.

The network had gone to a lot of effort to get this show filmed despite the black cloud that had formed over it. Stepping into Darcy's immensely talented shoes with a subpar cameraman, a nervous crew, and contestants who had been traumatized previously had kept her awake many nights.

All she could do at this point was her absolute best. With a couple of hours of daylight left, she could at least get the lay of the land. Check out the facilities and start to map out a general idea of how to set up the working stage area.

Rylie wandered over to a large barn several hundred feet behind her cabin. There were half a dozen cabins aside from hers and the office building. They all appeared to be empty and in need of a little love and attention. The barn had a shiny green metal roof and gray metal siding. Obviously newly constructed, it stuck out among all the other more rustic structures.

Massive double doors rose up before her. Grasping the handle of one, she pushed it to the right. As the door slid open, overhead lights turned on, flooding the huge space with fluorescent light.

Immediately to her right was a large closet or maybe an office. It had one window with a drawn blind and a deadbolt on the door. To the left sat a lawn tractor, a couple wheelbarrows, and some other equipment. Rows of floor-to-ceiling shelving lined the other three walls. Rylie stepped inside and checked out the shelves closest to her on the left. Each one had a neatly labeled sign listing what could be found on the shelf in question. She found labels for tents, fire building, sleeping bags, cooking gear— and that was just in one area.

As Rylie scanned the items, she caught a hint of movement in a shadowy corner. Ignoring all the warnings her brain issued in super quick succession, the sound of a window sliding open drew her in that direction. As she approached, she glimpsed a pair of faded jeans and worn sneakers disappearing through the open window. Jogging over, she peered out and saw a figure running away toward the woods.

Going over to where she'd seen the movement, Rylie peered behind one of the shelves. A sleeping bag had been shoved into a corner, and an empty water bottle along with a couple food wrappers littered the area.

"Are you looking for anything in particular?"

The deep, bellowing voice filled the barn, causing Rylie to startle. She jumped out of the corner, reluctant to let her host know that someone had been stowed away in his barn just yet.

"Do you always sneak up on people like that?" She turned to face Carter, straightening herself up to her full five feet and nine inches, determined to appear more calm, cool, and collected than she was.

"Do you always snoop around private property?" Carter glared at her, his sullen mood emanating from him in waves. It was beyond obvious that he did not want her on his mountain.

Or maybe he was embarrassed about seeing her nearly naked not long before.

"We have a contract that states I can use all buildings and equipment needed to film." She propped her hands on her hips. "You're being well compensated by the network for this, don't forget."

Carter's glare morphed into a scowl. "Ah, yes, the contract. How could I forget the network and their money?" He waved a hand in the air. "Is there something in particular you need to use for your *filming*?"

His annoyance aggravated her. "No one forced you to agree to this, you know. In fact, I thought you offered the property up for use."

He stared at her so long, it made her squirm. "You don't know anything about me or my reasons for agreeing to this silly show. Just stay out of my way, and I'll try to stay out of yours. If you need something from here, see me or Josh. Don't help yourself, or we'll have no way to monitor inventory."

Carter turned on his heel and stomped away.

"You weren't so worried about staying away from me thirty minutes ago!"

Carter didn't reply; he just stomped harder as he left the barn.

Waiting until she was certain he would be gone from the area, she walked out of the barn and pulled the heavy door closed. Continuing on her walk, Rylie headed down a dirt road labeled with a post-and-board sign painted bright red that had *Campsites* etched on it and an arrow pointing into the trees.

The first campsite she encountered had a firepit made from stones and a worn wooden picnic table that probably had a lot of stories to tell. A flattened area gave the appearance that many tents had been set up there over the years. No hookups for water or electricity anywhere in sight. The campground definitely had that rustic thing going on.

The next three campsites were similarly arranged with only a couple hundred feet between them. Maybe half a mile into her trek, she encountered a series of four outhouses and an old-fashioned water pump with a shiny red handle. Rylie smiled. Definitely no amenities at the Blue Ridge Mountains Campground and Survival School.

A fork in the dirt track boasted another sign.

This one indicated more campsites to the left and the presence of a small waterfall to the right. Rylie chose the path toward the waterfall. It had been a really long time since she'd done any hiking in the Blue Ridge Mountains. They were filled with the beautiful scenery of streams, creeks, and waterfalls. She'd never admit this to anyone else, but lately she'd been a bit homesick for the peace and beauty of the mountains. Living in Los Angeles had been exciting for a while with its huge ocean beaches, Hollywood stars on pretty much every corner, and a nightlife like nothing she'd ever dreamed of. But it had all gotten kind of old. Especially after losing her closest, and pretty much only, friend.

Getting her big break in television had been beyond tough. Years of *"Yes, sir"* and *"Yes, ma'am"* to outlandish demands, ridiculously long hours, and poverty-level pay had been grueling, even with the fantastic boss she'd had in Darcy. When the network had originally agreed to the show Darcy pitched, Rylie jumped at the chance to go home for a while. Her soul longed for crystal-clear water, air that wasn't heavy with exhaust, and blue skies as far as the eye could see. Being here now, without Darcy, felt all sorts of wrong, though. *Survive This* had been *her* dream, not Rylie's.

As she walked, Rylie took in the sounds and smells of the woods surrounding her. A large owl perched high in a tree called out to an invisible mate, and a murder of crows cawed as they circled above some dead animal they were about to feast on. About five minutes into her trek, the low rumble of rushing water reached her. After she walked a few hundred feet more and around a bend, she encountered a beautiful fall of mountain water sliding over age-smoothed rocks and crashing into a small pool a hundred or so feet below.

It had been far too long since she'd witnessed such a magnificent feature of nature. Rylie inhaled deeply, letting the cool fall air saturate her lungs. LA had nothing on the beauty of the Blue Ridge Mountains. It was just the balm her aching heart needed to begin to heal.

The sun had begun to set, hanging so low in the fall sky that more shadows than light surrounded her. Reluctant to leave but knowing she had to, Rylie turned and headed back the way she'd come. Somehow she'd work that waterfall into the show production.

"Welcome home, girl," she murmured. "This is exactly where you need to be."

A shiver passed down her spine as gooseflesh

prickled along her arms. Rylie glanced around, unable to shake the feeling of being watched. Seeing nothing but trees with rustling leaves and a squirrel on a branch chattering at her animatedly, she tried to push the odd chill away by rubbing her hands up and down her arms. Moving faster to try and beat the setting sun as much as to escape the creepy feeling, Rylie practically jogged back to the main area. Her stomach growled loudly, reminding her that it had been way too long since her last meal.

"I wonder what mountain men eat for dinner." Picturing Carter with a spit over a fire, roasting a squirrel or maybe a rattlesnake, had her laughing out loud.

The man was a mystery. One minute cordial and maybe even friendly. The next? An angry recluse with a chip the size of one of his cabins on his shoulder.

CHAPTER THREE

CARTER DID HIS BEST TO STAY IN THE SHADOWS. He wasn't about to let his guest know that she'd discovered *his spot*. The place he retreated to when he needed to escape the craziness of his world. With any luck, she'd just forget about it and never go back there again.

He had a feeling his luck wouldn't hold out on that, though. It was far too beautiful and would be a major resource for the show's cast members.

For half a second, he'd almost felt bad about snapping at her in the barn until he overheard her refer to him as a mountain man. The way she'd laughed certainly didn't seem like it was a good thing. It evoked images of a caveman wearing a lion's skin loincloth, eating raw meat with his hands, and that annoyed the heck out of him. Did she actually see him that way?

The bigger, more important question—why did he even care how she saw him?

At least she'd changed her clothes into something more practical for camping. Rylie Christianson looked a whole lot better in her current attire than she had in that ridiculous getup she'd arrived in. He got the feeling she was far more comfortable now as well. Not that he didn't feel a little bad about her dress tearing the way it did.

He'd also be lying if he didn't say it had definitely accentuated all her curves. In fact, it looked like it had been made just for her. His body tensed at the memory of her lying on top of him with that dress on.

The glimpse he'd gotten of her through the bathroom window when he was headed to the barn—he got embarrassed all over again just thinking about the unexpected encounter—confirmed what the dress had hinted at.

If his mama had caught him acting like a damned peeping Tom....

What the holy hell was wrong with him? He should accept responsibility and apologize for the mistake.

Except... he wasn't too certain he was all that sorry about it.

A loud rumble sounded from his gut. It had been a long time since lunch. Maybe it was low blood sugar that had him all out of sorts.

It couldn't possibly be a green-eyed brunette with legs for days messing with his head—and body.

Rylie Christianson was totally not his type.

If he told himself that enough times, he might actually believe it.

He could never subject anyone to the huge mess he'd become anyway.

Nope.

Carter only had one focus—getting his survival school up and running full-time. Love was too messy.

Someone else's messy relationship had led to his entire world getting turned upside down. Nothing good ever came of being vulnerable. He'd seen that up close and personal firsthand, and he'd nearly died in the process.

Now that he'd been forced to focus on it, his business would be all-encompassing for a long time. Distractions of any kind, like hosting a glorified game show, were bad. If the money from the network wasn't absolutely essential for finishing his business plan, Carter would never have offered up the land.

Not even to assuage the heavy guilt he carried on his shoulders all the time.

The walk back to the cabin area took him only a few minutes despite the sun having pretty much set already. He knew the path and most of his property like he knew the lines on the palm of his hand, every trail and landmark established in his brain. For two years he'd dreamed of making the land into a premier primitive survival school, and the arrangement with Rylie and her network was all he needed to make those dreams a reality.

As long as he could survive the next three weeks of filming and strangers in his private space. Three weeks of the citrusy scent and the long chestnut hair of Rylie Christianson invading his personal space and taking up valuable real estate in his brain.

He let out a heavy sigh.

Too many long, sleepless nights had to be messing with his head.

Love and romance and marriage and families weren't for him. His brothers were sappy enough for the entire town. Let them deal with the eventual heartbreak that always came with love.

He'd just spent more time than he should have talking himself out of an attraction to Rylie.

Carter grunted and kicked at a loose rock on the ground. He had to be losing his entire mind.

Rounding the last bend into the large area littered with cabins, the soft wash of light from the only outdoor lamps on the property felt like a welcome home. Across the clearing, he could see Rylie heading to the cabin he'd assigned to her.

It was the nicest hooch in the place. He wanted the hotshot city-girl producer to be as happy as possible to make sure there were no glitches in the contract. He *wanted* that money more than he'd wanted pretty much anything else in his life to date.

Yup, it was all about the money.

Liar!

Ignoring his inner voice, Carter forced himself to look away.

Law enforcement had lost its luster since the incident that changed his entire career and life. Having to give it up wasn't the heartbreaking experience he'd thought it would be. He craved peace and quiet and a life free of crime and stress. If the ridiculous reality show about to be made on his property was the price he'd have to pay, then so be it. He could just keep his distance and let them do their thing.

Carter's stomach rumbled again. He really

needed to eat and probably feed his guest as well. Josh had long since left, so it would only be the two of them until her camera guy got here.

"Ms. Christianson!" he called to her.

She stopped moving, resting her hand on the doorknob as she turned to look at him. He took a few strides, closing the distance between them.

"I prefer Rylie, if you don't mind." The warmth she'd shown earlier had definitely cooled. Her voice echoed the lack of emotion in her eyes.

Carter gave her a nod. "Yes, ma'am. Sorry about that."

She frowned. "I prefer Rylie over Ms. Christianson *and* being called *ma'am*. I am definitely not old enough for that."

He felt the heat rise up his neck and onto his face. "Sorry again, ma'—um, Rylie. Mama would have my hide for being disrespectful if she were here. Old habits sometimes die hard."

A slow smile spread across her lips, instantly warming her green eyes. "I guess I've been living in LA too long. Sometimes I forget country courtesy. Rylie is just fine, though—seriously. No *ma'am* necessary."

Was he mistaken, or had he caught the slightest hint of an accent similar to his own? There was something about her—something that called out her city life as all wrong.

"You got it, Rylie. If I slip up, though, just smack me upside the head or somethin'."

The hot flush of embarrassment washed over him. His own mountain drawl got thicker when he was nervous or stressed. At the moment, he could have paved a road with the words rolling off his tongue, the drawl was so bad. That had to be the stress of the show. It couldn't possibly be the beautiful woman standing not ten feet away from him.

She studied him curiously. "Was there something that you wanted, Mr. Marshall?"

Something foreign happened—something he'd about forgotten he knew how to do—as a smile slowly spread over his own lips.

Damn it. She had him smiling?

"Please, just call me Carter."

Rylie flashed another lovely smile at him, melting a little more of the ice in his chest. "Was there something you wanted, Carter?"

The loudest rumble of the evening so far sounded from his abdomen. Embarrassment flooded through him as Rylie laughed heartily.

Ignoring his desire to crawl under the nearest rock and stay there for the next month, he laughed a little too.

CAROLYN LAROCHE

A rusty, strained sound but a laugh nonetheless. "As my stomach is trying to tell you, I'm heading to the dining hall to make a little supper if you'd like to join me."

"I need about ten minutes to take care of a few things, but then I'd love to. I'm absolutely famished. It's been a crazy long day."

Carter nodded. "Me too. I'll head over and see what I can rustle up for us. I haven't been to the supermarket in a while, so no promises on the level of gourmet. Unless my brother managed to slip a few things into the walk-in when I wasn't looking."

Rylie laughed. "I'm so hungry right now, gnawing bark off a tree is starting to sound good. Hit me with whatever you've got."

"I tell you what. Give me twenty minutes, then head on over." Carter pointed at a low building that resembled the barn in structure but had a much less impressive stature. "That's where I'll be. Just follow the scent of bachelor in a kitchen and you'll find me."

She chuckled. "Bachelor in a kitchen? What's that smell like?"

"I suppose you're about to find out." With a quick nod, Carter turned on his heel and headed toward the dining hall.

Holy hell. Was he just *flirting*?

When he heard the door to Rylie's cabin click shut, he glanced over his shoulder to where they had just been. His gut told him to double-check that she was safely inside.

A rustle in the trees stopped him in his tracks.

"It's just an animal. The woods are full of them," he murmured, not at all convincing himself as he slowly scanned the tree line in the dim light. Something felt... off. He pulled out his cell phone, turned on the flashlight function, and slowly ran the beam of light across the area where he thought the sound had come from. He reached with his other hand for the phantom gun on his hip out of habit. He'd stopped carrying after the incident that nearly cost him his life.

All the tension of that night suddenly flooded through him. Adrenaline pumped up his heart and sent blood and anxiety coursing through his body. A light sheen of perspiration formed on his skin despite the coolness of the evening air. Carter opened and closed the fist of his former gun hand as he took several deep breaths.

Fight or flight? His nervous system couldn't seem to decide as his muscles tightened and his brain yelled at him to get the hell out of there.

Another rustle almost sent him running. Suddenly a rabbit hopped its way out of the brush.

"See? It was an animal," he said aloud in an effort to convince himself all was well. Carter exhaled the deep breath he'd been holding and continued on to the kitchen. By the time he reached the dining hall building, his heart rate had settled down some, and he relaxed a little bit. He hated how much spooked him now. He felt light-years away from the man he was not so long ago.

As he pushed the double doors open, a loud crash sounded from the back of the kitchen area, followed by the slamming of a door. He froze briefly, unsure what to do. Instinct took over, and Carter raced toward the noise. The kitchen was dark, so he flipped on the lights, something he wouldn't have done as a cop. Carter let out a loud string of all his favorite cuss words, plus a few extras for emphasis.

Complete chaos greeted him. Pots and pans were strewn everywhere. Ketchup and mustard had been squirted across every shiny surface. The perpetrator had made sure to get every single countertop, the griddle, and the gas stove. An entire bottle of syrup had been emptied onto one counter and then coated in a thick layer of flour. Someone had written the letters *F U C* followed by a swiped handprint. A large stack of previously clean plates lay in a shattered mess on the floor as well—most likely the crash he'd just heard.

He grabbed a flashlight from a shelf over the drying rack and switched it on as he ran out the back door. Flour-coated footprints led away from the delivery area, disappearing into the trees.

What in the actual hell had just happened to his kitchen?

And why?

The only people who should be on the mountain were him and Rylie—and he had literally just watched her enter her cabin.

Actually, no, he hadn't.

He *heard* the door close but wasn't looking at the time.

It didn't make any sense, though. Why would Rylie vandalize his facility when she needed it for her television show? The answer was easy—she wouldn't. She'd have to have superhuman powers to get there ahead of him anyway.

That meant someone else was on the mountain with them.

He squatted down and studied the footprints left in the soft dirt outside the door a little more closely. With the flashlight, he could clearly make out a pattern. They definitely indicated a common sneaker print that he'd seen many times before. If he had to guess, they were a men's size eleven or twelve.

"Carter? Are you here?" Rylie's voice carried through the kitchen and out the door to where he still squatted, now taking a few photos of the prints. "What happened? Are you okay? Carter!"

He rose to his full height and yelled through the open door, "Hold on, I'll be right there!"

Making his way back through the mess, Carter met up with Rylie near the long serving counter between the kitchen and the dining area. She stood still, gaping at the disarray.

Looking over at him, she frowned. "Um, did you have a little trouble trying to decide what to make us for dinner? I told you, I'm not a picky eater. A peanut butter sandwich would have sufficed."

The look on her face—utter confusion colored with a bit of curiosity—was more humorous than it should have been. He chuckled as he shook his head. "This wasn't me."

"Then what happened?" She pulled her phone from the back pocket of her jeans. "Does 911 work up here?"

"I chased an intruder out the back door. They're

probably halfway down the mountain by now. I'm not going to report it."

Her confusion switched to a hint of fear. "I thought we were the only ones up here."

Carter shrugged. "We are. Or we're supposed to be. I'm guessing maybe a homeless person or a teenager out to cause a little trouble. There's been a spree of vandalism in the area the past few months. It's also possible that I have an old enemy from when I was on the job."

"Seriously?" Rylie looked around the room. "Someone got mad over a speeding ticket and drove all the way up here to do this? For what—revenge? Way to hold a grudge for far too long."

He suspected this was over more than a traffic stop but didn't want to worry his guest. "I'm sure someone thought the place was empty. My interrupting his handiwork was probably punishment enough."

"I mean, if you say so. You're the cop."

Carter grunted. "Ex-cop."

She shrugged. "Whatever you say." Rylie's glance settled on the syrup message, and then she looked at him, a hand clapped over her mouth. "I totally forgot until now!"

"Forgot what?" Carter asked as he pulled out his

phone and snapped several pictures of the mess and damage in case he ended up making an insurance claim. Though he had no intention of calling the police department for a report this time, he still wanted to document what had happened if the vandal returned. Carter preferred to limit contact with his former place of employment if he could.

"When I was in the barn earlier, I'm pretty sure I saw someone climbing out a window."

Carter stopped taking pictures to look at her. "What? Why didn't you say anything?" Anger flooded him as he glared at her.

She shrugged. "I don't know. It didn't seem like a good time, I guess."

"A good time!" he bellowed. "Someone climbed out a window to avoid being found, and you didn't think it was a good time to mention to me that there was a potential perp in my barn?"

She held her hands up in surrender. "Sorry. I didn't want to poke the bear if I didn't have to."

Something changed inside him as his stance relaxed. He chose his next words carefully. "I *always* want to know about anything out of the ordinary on my property, okay?"

Rylie nodded. She stayed out of his way as he

worked but didn't leave. He felt her watching him intently, deep in thought about something.

When he'd finished snapping photos, he set his phone down on one of the only clean shelves by the griddle. He had to eat. Judging by the wave of hangry he felt, it couldn't be postponed any longer.

"You ready for some food?" he asked.

"I thought you'd never ask." Rylie grinned and rubbed her abdomen. "It's been way too many hours since I last ate. Did you know they don't even give out peanuts on planes anymore? In case someone is allergic."

She did a good job of hiding her concern about the vandalism while he cooked. Little worry lines on her forehead gave her away, though. As she rambled on about the craziness of her flight from LA, Carter surveyed the griddle. It was a mess but not nearly as bad as he'd first thought when he entered the kitchen.

Carter stepped around Rylie where she leaned against a counter, intending to grab a scrub brush. As he tried to get by, the space between the woman and the counter was just a tiny bit too narrow to avoid touching her. The electricity that had threatened to erupt earlier mounted into a full-blown shock wave of something he hadn't experienced in a very long time. Inhaling deeply to reclaim his composure, Carter averted his eyes.

"Let me clear off the griddle, and I'll make us some omelets and toast."

"Ah yes, the single man's staples." Rylie's green eyes danced with humor. "I bet you make omelets for all the girls."

Had she felt the same electric jolt he had?

Carter ran a wet towel over the griddle, creating a tie-dye effect with the condiments. Grumbling, he hit it with a second wet towel and then the cleaning brush. Rylie's joke struck a tight chord within him. A chord that reminded him it had been a very long time since there'd been any reason to cook for someone else.

"Actually, no other woman has ever been in this kitchen with me. Except Mama, but she did the cooking." He flipped the knob to On, and then he sprayed the heating surface with some clean water and used the scraper to push the remaining slop into the grease trap. "I suppose that will make you the envy of all the locals. I'm a man of mystery around here. There'll be plenty of gossip come the weekend."

"I find that very hard to believe." Rylie leaned against a counter that hadn't been completely sabotaged. "I'm sure all the women in town would line up for a taste of your... omelets."

She gave him a sly little grin. Carter's flirting skills were as rusty and frozen as the Tin Man in *The Wizard of Oz* when Dorothy found him alone in the forest.

Unsure how to respond, he busied himself prepping the now-clean grill. Without making eye contact, he asked, "Can you grab the eggs from the walk-in? There should be a big bag of shredded cheese as well. And any veggies you can find. I'm not really sure what's in there, to be honest. My brother may actually have done some shopping."

Without a word, Rylie made her way to the walk-in cooler. She moved gingerly, avoiding slick spots on the floor. He hoped he hadn't hurt her feelings with his inadequate social skills, but he suspected he had.

With yet another heavy sigh, he greased up the griddle and waited for Rylie to return with the omelet ingredients.

CHAPTER FOUR

CARTER REMINDED HER OF AN EIGHTY-YEAR-OLD recluse who hadn't gone out in public for forty years. Awkwardness defined every interaction they had. Relating to another human on, well, a human level appeared to be quite difficult for him.

She'd struggled endlessly with what had happened to Darcy. Rylie suspected that Carter had as well.

When she entered it, she found the walk-in cooler almost empty. A case of eggs sat on one rack, the five-pound bag of shredded cheese right next to it, and there was an onion and a bag of spinach on another shelf. That pretty much summed up the contents.

Rylie grabbed it all and returned to where Carter stood.

"Do you only eat eggs?" she asked, unloading her finds on the stainless steel counter beside the griddle.

Carter shrugged. "It's easy and filling. I don't put a lot of thought into what I eat as long as it fixes my hunger."

He dropped a pat of butter on the griddle and moved it around until it melted. After cracking three eggs into a bowl, he whipped them lightly with a fork, then poured them onto the hot surface. As the eggs cooked, Carter formed them into a nearly perfect circle. His meticulous process fascinated her. He quickly diced some onion and set that to sauté with a handful of spinach beside it.

Everything he did, every move he made, was perfectly choreographed as though he actually did eat omelets at every meal. As the scents of the different ingredients wafted up and mingled in the space around them, her mouth literally began to water. The man doing the cooking didn't look so bad either and might very well have added to her hunger.

Carter caught her watching him and raised an eyebrow in question.

She immediately reached up to touch her chin, then giggled. "Am I drooling?" *Please don't let me be drooling*. "Because that smells so darn good. Not to mention, you're fun to watch when you cook." He flipped the eggs and sprinkled them with a generous amount of cheddar cheese. Rylie licked her lips—purely for the food, she hoped.

Carter narrowed his eyes at her. "Is this really that entertaining?"

She laughed, partly due to nerves and partly because she probably looked and sounded ridiculous. Why not add insult to injury? "I love watching a man cook. Tells me they were raised right."

Carter actually chuckled. "Mama used to say no son of hers wouldn't know his way around a kitchen. And since I have four brothers, we got a lot of lessons and a lot more practice. You should see what I can do with a steak and a potato. Every one of us has a bit of skill. Two of my brothers worked in restaurants for a few years before switching to law enforcement. Personally, I think she did it so she wouldn't have to feed five teen sons and a husband by herself every night."

He seemed so relaxed talking about his mother and his brothers. Completely different from the gruff man she'd encountered in the barn. "That sounds like an offer for another meal tomorrow. I'm definitely a steak-and-potatoes girl."

The words slipped so easily from her lips that she had absolutely no opportunity to even try to hold them back. She didn't really want to anyway. The thought of another meal with Carter Marshall appealed to her far more than she'd expected.

Carter plated the food and handed it to her without making eye contact. "I popped some bread in the toaster when you went to the walk-in. I heard it pop a minute or so ago if you want to go grab it."

Rylie accepted the meal, her stomach loudly growling its thanks. He raised an eyebrow as she shrugged. "I haven't actually eaten since breakfast. This smells and looks amazing. Thank you."

"You really shouldn't skip meals." Carter cracked four eggs onto the griddle and repeated the entire omelet-making process.

"Coming from a man who apparently lives on eggs and cheese. When did you eat last?" She took a bite of the omelet and moaned. "Holy hell, this is amazing."

He didn't look over at her, but she saw his lips twitch a bit, as though he was holding back a smile. "I may not have a varied diet, but I rarely miss a meal. Based on how impressed you are with these eggs, I'm guessing you eat a lot of cereal?"

"Aren't you the funny one." Rylie set her dish

down, buttered two slices of the toast, and piled half her eggs onto one piece. She picked it up and bit into the open-faced sandwich. Breadcrumbs rained down on her shirt, covering her chest in toasted fairy dust. On the second bite, the bread split in half, dumping several big chunks of cheesy eggs down her front.

"Darn it!" Little bits of partially chewed food came spraying out her mouth, several landing on Carter's arm and the hot grill he cooked on. "Someone, please just kill me now before the embarrassment takes me!"

Dropping the plate onto the counter with a loud clatter, she grabbed a dish towel and tried to mop up the mess she'd just made but only succeeded in making a bigger one.

Carter chuckled as he plucked a few pieces of egg off her shirt. Rylie froze. The unexpected contact between them turned the temperature up in the kitchen instantly.

What on earth was wrong with her? Heat rose quickly up her neck and spread over her face. Perspiration literally dripped from her palms.

"I'm so sorry. Sometimes I am just so—" As she reached over to clean the chewed bits off his arm, the entire building went dark. Rylie missed Carter's forearm and fell toward the griddle. As the fingers of her left hand made contact with the edge of the hot surface, she let out a yelp. At the same time, strong hands gripped her waist, lifting her off the ground and spinning her away from the cooking surface before both palms—or worse, her chest and face—landed on the griddle.

As he pinned her between him and the prep counter, Carter's breaths were hot against her cheek. He held a finger to her lips. "Shhh.... Are you hurt?" he asked, his voice low and gruff against her ear.

Rylie shook her head. "Just lightly singed the tips of a couple of my fingers. I think you grabbed me in time."

The sound of shattering glass filled the air.

"What was that?" she whispered.

"I think someone broke a window in the dining area." Wishing he hadn't set the flashlight down earlier, Carter turned his phone's flashlight on, then reached over and grabbed a very large knife from the magnet on the wall. "Give me your good hand."

She did as he said.

"Take this knife and follow this counter to the office. If anyone comes at you, cut them." Carter stepped away from her. "I'll be back as soon as I can. The drawer in the office has a flashlight in it. Make your way there and lock yourself in. Don't open it until I tell you to, no matter what you hear."

"Let me come with you. I'll watch your back." Rylie's whole body trembled, and her heart was racing from the double dose of adrenaline, but she wanted to put up a brave front for the man who had just saved her from third-degree burns.

"Go. Now." He turned her body in the right direction and gave her a gentle push toward what she expected to be the office. "I can't protect you and find who's trying to destroy my property at the same time."

Before she could say another word, he disappeared out the back door into the night.

Rylie, moving extra cautiously and listening for any sign of another person in the kitchen, made her way to the office like Carter told her to. Normally, she'd balk at a man commanding her to do anything. Her instincts told her to follow his instructions, though, so she did.

When she got to the office, Rylie pulled the door closed and turned the lock. The fingers on her left hand burned and throbbed, but she barely noticed thanks to the continuous flow of adrenaline still coursing through her.

The room was so small, she basically turned from

the door right into the side of the desk, banging her toes hard against a leg. "Ouch!"

Clapping her injured hand over her mouth to stifle the cry, she winced at the pain in her fingers. Carefully setting the knife down on the surface of the desk, she followed around the piece of furniture to what she assumed to be the front when her knee hit a chair.

Stifling yet another outburst of pain, she felt around for a drawer. When her fingers made contact, she pulled it open and reached in for the flashlight.

When she finally had it in her hand, she clicked the switch. The small space was illuminated immediately. Scanning the room, she discovered a small window directly across from the door.

Settling down in the chair, Rylie turned the light back off. She strained to hear anything that might give her a clue as to whether Carter was okay or not. The exaggerated silence unnerved her.

After what seemed like forever, footsteps sounded in the kitchen. A few seconds later, a glow of light shone from under the door, telling her the electricity had been restored. Rylie exhaled a long breath she hadn't realized she'd been holding.

"Rylie?" Carter's voice passed through the closed door, calming her instantly. "You can come out now."

She jumped from the chair and leaped toward the door, turning the lock and yanking it open. Carter stood there, looking far more relaxed than she felt.

"Is everything okay?"

He actually offered up half a smile. "Come on out. I want you to meet someone."

His casual demeanor confused her, especially after he'd basically told her to stab anyone who tried to hurt her a few minutes earlier.

Rylie followed him from the office and over to the serving counter. A young teenager stood there, a scowl firmly in place. The boy had his head hung low, long hair well past needing a cut and a shampoo creating a curtain around his face. She couldn't help but notice the level of wear his jeans and tennis shoes had withstood and that his once-black hoodie had faded to a washed-out gray. Several holes had worn through the hem. This boy had not been well cared for, and it hurt her heart.

"Rylie, this is Jay. We last met last year when I arrested him for tagging the side of the public library with some inappropriate language. He decided to get a little revenge tonight. Isn't that right, Jay?"

The teen ignored the question, kicking the toe of his shoe against the leg of a prep table.

"You want I should just call someone to take you in? I still got dispatch on speed dial." Carter's voice had grown gruffer, showing his annoyance.

"It seemed like a good idea at the time. But you really can't hold me responsible."

"And why not?" Carter looked at him, obviously curious.

"My science teacher says my frontal lobe hasn't developed all the way and I am not capable of always making good choices." The boy looked so serious that Rylie nearly laughed out loud.

"Well, Jay, I hope you know now that it was *not* a good choice," she said. "Mr. Marshall is a good man, and if he arrested you, it was because you were breaking the law—not because he's a big jerk. Well, sometimes I bet he is, but not then."

"Now wait just a minute." Carter turned on her, but she gave him a little wink. He backed off, but she could tell it wouldn't last if they kept pushing his internal buttons.

Jay scowled and shifted his weight. "Yeah. He was kinda nice to me when he arrested me back when he was a cop."

Carter crossed his arms over his chest in a very police officer way as something dark briefly passed over his expression. "I may not be a cop anymore, but you've gone and committed a second felony, Jay. Actually, multiple felonies. All this damage adds up. Technically, this could get your ROR for good behavior revoked. They'll lock you up in juvie for it."

Jay snapped his head up, eyes wide with fear and all hint of attitude gone. "You'd do that?"

Carter shrugged. "Give me one reason why I shouldn't take you to the station right now and have them book you. Because I'll give you at least two thousand dollars' worth of reasons why I should."

He scowled again. "My old man's gonna kill me this time for certain. Come on, bruh. You *saw* him last time. *Please* don't tell him."

Surely Carter wouldn't put this boy in harm's way intentionally.

"Actually, you know what? I'll be safer in juvie if you tell him. So you may as well just lock me up."

Rylie was about to speak up in the boy's defense when Carter's entire stance seemed to relax. His expression remained stern, but he didn't look like he wanted to wrestle an alligator anymore.

"I suppose I could let you work the debt off. Clean up the mess you've made and then work around here for a month or two after school and on weekends until the broken window and dishes have been paid for."

Jay's hardened expression filled with a little hope. "You'd do that?"

Carter unfolded his arms and gestured around the room. "You've got a lot of damage to make up for. It won't be easy. I'm talking chopping-and-stacking-wood level hard."

"I'm strong. I might look scrawny, but I can handle hard work. No better workout than fighting my pop when he's knee-deep in a bottle of whiskey."

If Rylie weren't mistaken, Jay almost seemed excited to do the work despite the annoyed expression he worked hard to maintain. Or maybe he was just happy to avoid being arrested.

Or, more likely, avoid being with his drunken father.

Whatever the reason, both he and Carter seemed satisfied with the arrangement, and Rylie could see that protective side of Carter she remembered from when they were in high school.

Carter leaned against a wall, hands shoved in his pockets. "If you don't hold up your end of the bargain, I'll bring the charges and drop you in juvie without a second thought."

"No worries, bruh. I said I'd do it."

There was so much more to this boy's story. So

much she didn't know, but she'd bet a year's salary that Carter knew every single detail.

Carter gestured around the kitchen once more. "You're gonna start now by cleaning up the condiment artwork and the broken glassware and dishes. When you're done, I'll drive you home."

A flash of fear passed over Jay's expression, but it disappeared so fast, Rylie couldn't be sure she'd actually seen it.

She decided to just outright ask him the question she'd been mulling over since Carter "caught" him. "Jay? Have you been sleeping in the barn?"

"What?" The boy looked confused. "No."

"Why would you think that?" Carter asked, also looking confused.

She shrugged. "I saw a sleeping bag on the floor in the corner when I was in there earlier."

Carter frowned. "And you neglected to mention that?"

"You were so busy chastising me for entering your precious space, I forgot." She glared at Carter, daring him to deny it.

Jay watched their exchange with interest. "You two married or something? You sound like the old people in the trailer next to ours."

"No!" Rylie and Carter blurted simultaneously, actually causing Jay to take a step back.

His expression blank, Carter stepped forward and steered the boy toward the closet that contained the cleaning supplies. "Get to work. It's getting late."

He frowned. "Okay, fine. But you don't gotta drive me back after. I can walk. My old man sees you bring me home, and it's gonna be on."

"It's too dangerous to walk on this mountain road even in the daylight. Forget about doing it at night," Rylie said.

He kicked at the floor with a worn-out sneaker. "I'll be fine. I walk around at night a lot. It's better than being home. Besides, you might have a flat tire on that truck of yours. You should be careful what you drive over."

Carter tensed up again. "What do you mean, I have a flat—"

"No worries," Rylie interjected. "He can take you back in my car. As long as all four tires are intact?" She gave him a questioning look. Jay nodded. "And tomorrow, when you come back to work, I'm sure you can change out the tire on Carter's truck."

Carter grunted. "Add that tire to the total you're going to be working off. Truck tires aren't cheap."

Jay raised an eyebrow. "That sweet little ride out there belongs to you?"

Rylie raised her own eyebrow in response. "What's that supposed to mean?"

The boy shrugged. "I figured you more for a Jeep girl or maybe some kinda old pickup truck. With a stick shift."

Images of her dated Ford Ranger parked in her driveway back in LA almost made her laugh out loud. The kid could read people.

The ridiculous red car had been her boss's idea. A way to peacock her feathers in front of the mountain folk and impress the contestants on the show, since so many had nearly backed out after Darcy's murder. She hated every inch of it but wouldn't admit that just yet.

"I guess you don't know much about city girls from California," Carter said before she could reply.

"How about you get to work cleaning up the mess you made." Rylie pointed to a broom propped in a corner of the kitchen. "It's like a minefield in here."

Carter nodded his agreement. "You know the way. There's a mop and bucket in the utility closet in the back of the room."

They watched as Jay strode toward the mess on

long, thin legs, his shoulders hunched forward as though he were trying to appear small.

Rylie turned to look up at Carter. "That's a nice thing you did."

He shrugged off the compliment. "I did myself a favor. I really didn't want to go to the station."

He headed toward the kitchen as well, leaving Rylie to contemplate everything that had just transpired. She and Carter had acted as a team. Suddenly it felt like she might have been brought here for a lot more than just to shoot a television pilot.

CHAPTER FIVE

Young Jay had tried to escape into the woods after smashing the dining hall window. Fortunately for Carter, his worn shoelace had come untied. Jay had tripped on it and landed spread-eagled in a pile of leaf debris, making it easy for Carter to pull him to his feet.

Jay had one of those sad stories like something shown on the news after a tragedy had happened. The neglect he received at the hands of his drunk father was criminal. At least in Carter's mind.

Still, the boy had done a lot of expensive damage, and he needed to make amends. Carter's choice to not bring him in had been partly selfish.

Not only would there be charges brought on Jay for the vandalism, but Carter would also catch a couple charges of his own for fighting Jay's old man when he laid hands on the boy. He and Brett Standish had gone toe to toe before—more than once. Only then, Carter had been on the job. Child Protective Services had failed the boy. No one could ever find a reason to remove him, but Carter knew better. His hands had been tied by his job, but not anymore. He had a choice about leaving the boy there or not.

A run-in with the older Standish now, though? Brett would press every charge the magistrate let him get away with. Not having Jay arrested protected them both.

The damage to the dining hall still had to be dealt with, though. Jay had to learn that he couldn't just destroy things when he got mad or frustrated. Especially a year later. That's when it becomes premeditated, not an emotional response.

Carter came up on Jay standing beside the flattop grill, holding the broom in one hand and the dustpan in the other. The eggs he'd been frying before the blackout had gone way past overcooked, yet the boy's mouth watered like he hadn't eaten in days.

"Find what you needed?" he asked Jay, breaking the spell holding him in a trance over the crispy mess on the grill.

The teen startled, dropping the dustpan. "Yeah, I'm good," he answered, bending to retrieve it.

He placed a hand on Jay's shoulder, turning the boy to face him. "When was the last time you had a meal, kid?"

Jay set to sweeping with a vengeance, clearing up shards of broken pottery. "A day or so, I guess. I, um, wasn't feeling so great. Sometimes I get lunch at school, though."

Carter sensed it had been way longer than the boy admitted to. He started cracking eggs into a bowl. When he'd added six of them, he used a whisk to whip them up some. Jay had stopped sweeping and began to watch.

"That's gonna be a big omelet," Jay commented.

"Yup." Carter tossed a pat of butter onto the hot surface and then poured the eggs slowly onto the newly scraped griddle, using the spatula to control the spread.

After melting some more butter on the hot surface, he added onion slices and a couple handfuls of spinach to the butter and began to toss it on the hot griddle. Jay's belly rumbled loudly.

"Um, it smells great," Jay mumbled, his face turning bright red with embarrassment.

Rylie chuckled, but Carter didn't respond at all.

He remembered how intense hunger during his teen years would wake him up even from a sound sleep. More than once, he raided the fridge at two in the morning, shoving shredded cheese or leftovers from dinner into his mouth. He never missed a meal or an excuse to eat; he couldn't imagine going *days* without food.

As Carter cooked, Jay side-eyed the food while sweeping up broken glass, but he didn't say anything. Rylie returned to eating her own meal as she also watched the entire scene with interest.

Carter stepped over to a cabinet and grabbed a small platter. After flipping the four pieces of toast, he then used the two spatulas to pick up the mound of food and placed it on the platter. With one spatula, he sliced each of the four pieces of toast and arranged them as a border on the platter. His own stomach rumbled as all the different scents surrounded him, but a quick glance at Jay showed the boy practically drooling. Carter pulled a fork from a drawer, then took the broom from Jay and replaced it with the plate of food.

"What? Now you want me to serve you your dinner?" Jay grumbled, his words an attempt to hide the hunger in his eyes.

It had so obviously been longer than he'd thought

since the boy had eaten. That kind of attitude mixed with desire only showed up when someone had been starving.

"I want you to put every crumb of that in your stomach. Then mop this place up so I can get you home. I'm an old man, and I need some sleep."

Jay's entire face filled with disbelief, softening his defensive stance. "You serious? This is all for me? It's too much." He tried to hand the dish back, but Carter shook his head.

"Go eat. I've got plenty here to whip some more up."

"This is totally dope." Jay headed to the dining area with his treasure, looking like a kid on Christmas morning. "For an old dude, you're not so awful."

"Gee, thanks," Carter grumbled as he reached for another egg and cracked it on the griddle. "He called me an old dude."

Rylie patted his arm. "It's okay, old dude. I can grab your walker for you if you need me to."

He glanced over at her, a frown marring his features. "Not you too."

"He breaks my heart." She motioned to Jay, whom they could see through the serving counter opening, devouring the plate of food. "I don't ever remember being so grateful for a meal."

"Yeah. There's a lot more food insecurity around here than people realize. Staunton might be growing, but the local mountain folk are still as poor as they were before rich people discovered the Blue Ridge Mountains." He grunted disapproval at his own words, then gestured toward the dining room. "Go eat with the kid. Make sure he doesn't try to run or something."

Rylie gave him a look that said, *I think we both know that boy isn't going anywhere.*

"Okay. As long as you promise to make yours next." She walked away as he cracked the next egg.

He'd gone way past hungry an hour ago. At this point, eating would just be purely functional.

After cracking four eggs and putting the toast on the grill for a couple of egg sandwiches, Carter stepped over to the still-open back door. As he stood there, letting the cool night air wash over him, a movement in the trees caught his eye.

"Hey, bear!" he called out, letting the common local animal know humans were in the area.

Normally, he'd hear crunching twigs and leaves as the bear meandered away. This time he heard nothing. Instead, he saw a flash of white in the trees. Something like a white shirt.

Stepping down onto the steps behind the door, he scanned the trees again. There! He saw it again.

"Who's out there?"

The only sounds answering him were the insects and birds of the night. Maybe hunger was actually getting to him, making him see things that weren't there.

Carter returned to the kitchen, closing the door behind him. He then did something he rarely did on his mountain—turned the lock.

By the time they'd all finished eating and cleaning up, Jay looked every bit the exhausted child he really was. Heavy eyelids fighting to stay open over watery eyes and a huge yawn totally gave his age away.

"You ready to go?" Carter asked the boy.

"You don't gotta take me home. I can just stay here." He patted the bench beside him. "Trust me, no one's gonna miss me for one night."

The plea in his words pulled at Carter—he wished he could let him stay, but Jay was technically a child out past curfew... among the other laws he'd broken that day.

"If you let me stay, I'll already be here for work. Sooner I get done and get out of here, the better."

"We need to get you home so your father doesn't worry." Rylie wrapped an arm around Jay's shoulders. He stiffened at her touch and sidestepped out of reach. She looked hurt but hid it quickly. "But you can come back after school tomorrow."

She delivered the words with a smile and the kind of gentleness Jay probably hadn't experienced in many years. He actually smiled back at her. "Tomorrow is Saturday, ma'am. No school. But I promise I'll be back bright and early."

The difference in the boy with Rylie versus the way he usually acted around Carter resembled the difference between night and day. Of course, Carter had usually taken him into custody for some dumb prank.

As they walked to Rylie's little car together, it surprised him how comfortable it all felt. A self-proclaimed loner, Carter had never dreamed of a wife and family the way his brothers had. He'd fully intended to spend his entire life alone and attachment free. He stayed so much safer that way. No heartaches. No disappointments.

As they approached the vehicle, Rylie sucked in her breath.

Carter saw what she did at the same time. "Stop. Both of you get behind me."

He scanned the area as best he could in the dim lights of the campground. "Jay? Did you go anywhere near Rylie's car today?"

"No, sir. Just yours." Carter caught the fear in his voice and believed him. "I swear I didn't touch hers at all. I wasn't mad at her."

Both doors of her car stood open, as did the trunk. Someone had taken the time to fill the interior with leaves, sticks, and other debris. Across the windshield, the word DIE had been painted in red. But the most disturbing part—the thing that had Carter wanting to lock Rylie and Jay in his cabin and tear the property apart—lay across the hood of the little coupe.

A large barn owl was draped over the surface, wings spread wide and an arrow—one of Carter's from the supply barn—through its heart. Its white feathers gave it a ghostly appearance under the floodlights. With the blood from the wound staining its gossamer breast, the owl looked every bit the nickname *demon owl* its particular species had been dubbed with.

"Rylie, can you take Jay back to your cabin? Lock

the door and keep the windows closed. I'm going to take a look around."

"Why don't we all go inside, and you can call 911 or something?" Rylie's voice had a tiny bit of uncertainty in it.

He turned to look at them. Rylie held the boy in a tight hug. He could feel their fear. "It's okay. Whoever did it is probably gone now anyway. I just need to be sure. Go inside and stay there until you hear me at the door, okay? Don't open it unless it's me. No matter what."

No need to mention the white flash he'd seen in the woods beyond the dining hall.

Jay looked over his shoulder at Carter, his fearful expression once again belying his age and the tough exterior he tried to uphold. "Don't get dead."

Carter's lips twitched a little despite the situation. The teen liked old movies. *Speed* had been one of his favorites back in the day.

"I won't. Now go."

Rylie led Jay quickly away. As soon as he knew they were safely locked in the cabin, Carter began to search. He pulled out his cell phone and took a picture of the bird and the car. Using the flashlight on his phone, he scanned the dirt for any sign of the intruder.

To his left, he spotted a partial print of what appeared to be some kind of tennis shoe. A few feet away he found another. The trail of prints led down the drive about fifty feet and then into the woods. If he tracked the perpetrator of the vile message, he'd be leaving two people unprotected.

But if he didn't go, the vandal would probably get away.

Knowing he had no choice, Carter trekked back up the drive and went straight to Rylie's cabin.

Tapping softly, he called through the wood, "It's me. Open the door."

When Rylie pulled it open, she held a finger to her lips. "Jay is asleep."

Curled up in the fetal position on the bed meant for Rylie, Jay looked more at peace than Carter had ever seen him in any of their previous interactions.

"He's just a child," Carter said softly. "He's normally so defensive and, honestly, a real jerk. I've never seen him so vulnerable."

"From what you both were saying earlier, it seems like maybe he has a story that is less than ideal." Rylie walked to the bed and pulled a faded patchwork quilt over Jay, then sat down in one of the two chairs in the main room.

Carter sat in the other chair across the tiny table

from her. "His mama died in a nasty car wreck. Slid off the road on her way home from work during one of the worst snowstorms we've ever had. She'd just gotten off the night shift as a nurse in the ER. Worked extra hours because of so many MVAs during the storm."

"MVAs?" Rylie asked.

"Oh, sorry—motor vehicle accidents." Carter ran his fingers through his hair. "Jay had been maybe five or six then. His daddy didn't take the news that he had to be a single father very well. Mourned his wife deep in a bottle. Still does. He's a violent, mean drunk too. He had his own mother living with them for a few years, but she died just after Jay turned twelve."

"The poor boy." Rylie shook her head sadly. "To essentially lose both his parents at the same time."

"He's been in one scrape after another since his grandmother died. She kept him in check and gave him attention." Carter sighed. "Unfortunately, we spent a good bit of time in my cruiser together over the last couple of years before I resigned. Trying to get the attention of his loser old man, I guess."

"I can't even begin to imagine what he's been through." Rylie glanced back through the opening to the bedroom. "Let him sleep. The sperm donor is probably passed out drunk by now anyway. I can keep an eye on him tonight."

Her use of the words *sperm donor* in place of *father* made him want to laugh, but he held back for fear of waking the boy.

Carter shrugged. "We're not going to be able to go anywhere anyway. My truck has a slashed tire, and your car is now a crime scene. I've got to call it in here in a minute. Not sure anyone will get up here tonight, though."

"Then it's settled. Jay can sleep here. I don't sleep much anyway—I'm kind of a night owl. I'll hang out here with him and do a little work while you take care of business."

"I'll be right outside. Keep the door locked and text me if you need anything." He held out a hand. "Give me your phone, and I'll put my number in."

"Here." She handed it over, and Carter typed his number in, then called himself.

He returned her cell phone. "Now I have your number as well. Remember, keep the door locked, and don't open it for anyone except me."

Rylie tapped her temple with a finger. "I got it, officer."

He shook his head. "Not an officer anymore. Anyway, I'll stay outside until Crime Scene and the detective get here. Keep an eye out just in case the guy returns. Do you have any idea who might have done that? Do you have any enemies?"

Rylie shrugged. "A lot of people know where I am. I can't imagine who I could have made an enemy of. I film reality shows—I don't do investigative reporting. Besides, the car is a rental. No one knows what I'm driving. My own vehicle is at home."

"If it was rented by the network, then anyone you work with would be able to find out." Carter walked over and looked out the one window in the room. "Someone has a grudge against you. A really big one."

"Is it possible the message was actually meant for you?" she asked.

He spun around to look at her, horror etched in all his features. "No one in this entire county would ever think such a... *car* belonged to me."

Rylie gave a little laugh. "I just thought I'd put the idea out there."

Carter cracked half a smile. "I'm going outside to call the station now. Text if you need anything, hear anything, or see anything."

She gave him a little salute with a teasing smile. "Yes, sir!"

CHAPTER SIX

DESPITE HIS BEST EFFORTS TO REMAIN unaffected by her, Carter found himself enjoying his interactions with the television producer. Her presence brought a little bit of light to the darkness he usually existed in. He also couldn't shake the feeling that he'd known her in the past. Yeah, she'd been the one to save him that day, but his gut told him it was something more than that.

Carter sat on a wide stump left over from a massive oak tree he'd removed when he purchased the land. It made a nice rustic seat, and he'd spent a good bit of time sitting there, thinking. Something about Rylie rang familiar to him in a way that went beyond that shooting.

Lani, the dispatcher, had dated one of his

brothers back in high school. She'd gotten pretty chatty when she found out he was the one calling. She had said it would be about thirty minutes until someone could get out there. There'd been a multi-vehicle accident on the Blue Ridge Parkway and a huge bar brawl at almost the same time. The accidents were common on the twisting mountain highway. Out-of-town folks took the turns too fast when they got caught up looking at the scenery or would try to take pictures while driving.

Bar brawls had become fairly common in recent years. However, this one had turned into yet another hostage situation. His gut clenched a little when she said that.

From what Lani told him, the perp and his girlfriend were holed up in the Travel Lodge across from the honky-tonk in downtown Staunton. Each time anyone tried to talk to him, he fired his gun. As his heart rate kicked up and he broke out in a cold sweat, his mind immediately went back to that day.

Lani said no one knew if the girlfriend was even still alive. A man in an adjoining room had been hit by one of the bullets and rushed to the hospital.

Carter knew it would take way longer than thirty minutes for anyone to get up to his campground.

So, he waited. Thirty minutes. Then an hour.

Two hours passed, and he did a quick perimeter check. The forest around him echoed with all the sounds of night in the woods, but there wasn't a single sound that could have been human. The earlier clouds had moved on, leaving a clear sky full of stars shining overhead. It also meant the air had a stiff chill to it. Off in the distance, an owl let out a sad call, maybe looking for its mate that quite possibly lay spread out on the hood of Rylie's car.

He'd checked on her and Jay about half an hour earlier. Rylie had fallen asleep in a chair, her head resting on a laptop on the small table. He then walked a few laps around the parking area while checking his phone a couple dozen times for a call or text.

The sky had begun to lighten on the horizon when he finally heard the sound of vehicles approaching. A Staunton police cruiser and the city crime scene van soon came into view. Thirty minutes had become three hours, and Carter felt it in every muscle of his cold, exhausted body.

"Hey, Marshall!" Vonda, the crime scene tech, called out as she climbed out of the van after she parked. The slightly eccentric woman had worked the night shift forever. A brilliant forensic scientist, she had a love of all things movies and regularly changed her hair color. This time she had bright blue streaks accenting her tight dark curls. "You piss off Clint Eastwood or something? Looks like someone went all *Gran Torino* on your car here."

"First of all, that is *not* my car. Second, I'm surprised to see you. I figured you'd be at the Travel Lodge."

"You act offended that I would think you'd drive something so... delicate." She shrugged into a white Tyvek suit. "It's gonna be awhile over there. Boss told me to run up here and see what you got, then go back."

He scowled at the tech, making her laugh. Vonda was well-known and mostly well-loved in the police department for her quick wit and even better skills working up a crime scene. He swore the woman could solve a serial arson with a single match and the thread off the hem of an old T-shirt.

The detective who had arrived with her remained in his car. From where Carter stood, he appeared to be on the phone.

She walked over to the car. "Oh, man! Poor owl. Looks like Hannibal Lecter had a fava bean salad tonight."

"What?" Carter asked, more than a little annoyed.

Vonda pointed at the bird's chest. "There's a cut next to the arrow. I'd bet a Diet Dr Pepper there's something missing. Something meaning the heart."

"I'd be willing to see your single Diet Dr Pepper and raise you a full case of cans that you just messed up a movie reference." Carter had finally caught her making a mistake, and he totally felt the need to point it out.

Vonda held up a hand. "Stop right there, officer. I said a fava bean salad. Not fava beans and a bit of chianti. Even Hannibal Lecter liked a little variety."

The door of the police cruiser opened, and the detective stepped out of the vehicle. "What's going on up here in your survival paradise, Marshall?"

Carter held back the natural grimace the other man always brought out in him. "Hey, Peters. I wish I could tell you. I've got a television producer here to film a reality show. She's the only one of her crew who showed up last night. It looks like some of Los Angeles followed her here, though."

The detective gave him a questioning look. "A reality show? You gonna have a bunch of college kids up here gettin' drunk and havin' wet T-shirt contests?"

Peters had been in some imaginary competition with Carter since back when they went through the academy together. He felt pretty confident that the other man threw a party the day Carter medically retired from the force.

"There's more than partying and getting half naked to reality television." Those were the exact words Rylie had said to him on the phone when he'd offered his property for filming, referring to his two simple rules—no skin and no partying on camera. His property was definitely all about nature, just not *that* kind.

Peters held up his hands in mock surrender. "Well, excuse the hell outta me, man. Looks like the drama is here anyway. Where's the owner of the car? I got some questions for her."

Carter shook his head. The Peters he'd always known had returned. "Relax, buddy. She's asleep in a cabin. Once the sun comes up, I'll take you over and introduce you. For now, let her and the kid sleep a little."

"She's got a kid, driving a sporty car?" Peters scratched his head in mock thought. "I suppose there's a certain appeal. She a MILF, Marshall?"

"You don't get out much, do ya, Peters?" The other man's tacky comments were definitely rubbing his cold, tired self the wrong way.

Peters scoffed. "I'm not the one with a MILF in a

cabin on a mountain. Seems a bit suspish to me. Are you her biggest fan?"

"I heard you, Peters!" Vonda called out. "Kathy Bates would be very offended."

"What are you talking about?" Peters shot back.

"If you tell me you've never seen the movie *Misery*...."

Carter did his best to control his annoyance at the banter. "Look. The kid isn't hers. You know Jay Standish?"

"The kid with a drunk for an old man?" Peters's lip curled up in a scowl.

He nodded. "Yeah, well, he was out wandering the mountain tonight and ended up here. We were heading out to give him a ride home when we discovered the owl and the rest of it."

Peters nodded in the direction of Carter's vehicle. "What's the matter with your truck?"

"It's got a flat, and I didn't want to have to change it until morning." Carter scowled. "Can you take your pictures and stuff so Vonda can do her thing and we can start cleaning this mess up?"

"I second the request!" Vonda hollered from where she was working at setting up her gear. "And for the record, Marshall doesn't date anyone! MILFs are more your style, Peter Pumpkin Eater."

"I hate when she calls me that," Peters muttered, his face turning crimson as he stomped over to the car.

Carter groaned. "Thanks for totally putting me out there, Vonda. You're a real peach."

"Hey, you know me. I call it like I see it. Always." She grinned as she pulled on some gloves and then readied the fingerprint dusting powder.

It didn't take long for Peters to make his notes and take photos.

The sun had just crested the tops of the trees when Rylie appeared at Carter's side. "Why didn't you wake me?"

"I thought I said not to leave the cabin," Carter snapped. He didn't mean to sound so gruff. Vonda wasn't exactly wrong about him not dating. In fact, he avoided all relationships anymore aside from his brothers. It had been a long time since he felt worried about someone. He didn't like feeling worried.

Seemingly completely unfazed, she smiled up at him. "The sun's up, you've got friends here working the scene, and it *is* my rental car. Pretty sure I should be here."

Carter scoffed, his feathers more than a little ruffled. People didn't usually question his judgment.

"Yeah, well, how do we know the guy isn't in the tree line with a bow and arrow, trying to get a shot off at you?"

Rylie laughed. "Then I think he would have taken his shot already, don't you?"

Peters caught sight of Rylie from his car. Waving, he stepped back out of the vehicle and meandered over to where they stood. Carter bit back a reply—for the moment anyway.

"Mornin', ma'am." Peters actually tipped his department-issue baseball-style cap at Rylie.

Carter couldn't hold back his laughter. "You John Wayne now or what?"

"I'd say he's more like the Sundance Kid!" Vonda said, laughing.

"Go back and pretend science matters in solving cases." Peters waved her off with a growl.

"It does a way better job than you do." Vonda always had quick return volley. It would serve the other man well to just back off.

Peters's face turned red as he started toward the crime scene tech. He was worse than a squirrel trying to protect his nuts—pun intended. Carter gave himself a silent point for such a creative dig as he redirected the man back to the case.

"Don't you have some questions for Rylie?"

Carter stepped in Peters's sightline to Vonda in an attempt to redirect the anger that had colored his expression.

Peters tapped his pen on his little pocket notebook. "As a matter of fact, I do. Ma'am, do you have any enemies you know of? A crazy ex, maybe? Someone whose toes you stepped on trying to break through a glass ceiling at work?"

Rylie pursed her lips and shook her head. "No crazy exes, and I haven't stolen anyone's promotion."

"So, who wants you dead?"

The blatant question obviously made Rylie uncomfortable.

"Peters...." Carter sent the man a warning look. "She just got here yesterday. No time to anger anyone in Virginia."

The detective gestured over to where Vonda carefully lifted the dead bird and placed it into a large box. "That bird tells a very different story, don't you think, Marshall?"

The echo of an engine working way too hard to climb up the steep drive to the campground filled the air.

Peters turned his attention to Carter. "You expecting someone else?"

Rylie spoke up. "I am. My cameraman and

production assistant. That's what I came out here to tell you. Jack texted to tell me he's almost here. I didn't want Sundance here to shoot him or anything."

Peters turned a dark shade of embarrassed at the reuse of Vonda's jab. "I think I have everything I need for now. I hope you'll be sticking around a bit in case I have other questions?"

"We'll be here three weeks," Rylie replied.

Vonda stood up from where she squatted, dusting for fingerprints at the back of the car, and shot them a huge grin. "You hear that? Three weeks, Peters. Think you can solve one case in three whole weeks? I know that's asking a lot and all."

Peters returned her grin with a scowl. "I can outwit your junk science any day. Nothing replaces good old-fashioned police work."

"If y'all are done comparing the sizes of your investigation tools, can we wrap this up? I've got a show to shoot." Rylie turned her back on them all as she waved at the driver of the SUV that had just crested the hill. Without another word, she walked away to greet her colleague.

At least Carter had assumed him to be her colleague, but by the way the man scooped Rylie up in a big bear hug, he couldn't actually be sure.

He also couldn't be too sure about the weird tug in the pit of his gut as he watched the man put Rylie back on her feet.

Peters had gotten back in his car and spun the tires a little as he peeled out down the drive. The other man might not have had the biggest "investigative tool," as Rylie had called it, but he sure knew how to *be* a real big tool.

CHAPTER SEVEN

A LITTLE PART OF RYLIE HOPED JACK'S GREETING had made Carter a tiny bit jealous. Normally, she wouldn't have allowed it, as she and Jack were colleagues, but for some reason, she'd wanted Carter to see it.

He'd watched them, his expression blank. His eyes, though? She could have sworn she'd caught a spark of something. The tension between them had run high from the moment she stepped out of her car the day before. It had nearly caused a break in the space-time continuum when she landed on him in the leaves. And who could forget the whole bathroom thing?

Bossy, overbearing, and frustrating—the man

made her crazy. Half the time she wanted to avoid him, but she also couldn't deny the heat that simmered between them whenever they made contact. He also had a heart of gold. Rylie saw the compassion in his eyes when Jay begged him not to turn him in and the protectiveness when Carter set a big platter of food in front of the very hungry boy.

Carter Marshall may have built a wall around his heart, but she knew from the way he fought for the hostages the day Darcy died that his icy exterior just needed some serious thawing.

Challenge received and accepted.

"Earth to Rylie." Jack tapped her shoulder. "Are you still with me?"

She smiled. "Sorry, it's been a long night. I guess I just spaced out for a minute."

"I really need to get unloaded and start working." He gave her a pointed look. "*We* need to get to work."

"I know, Jack." She grabbed a bag out of his trunk with a little more force than was probably necessary. "I said I'm sorry—it was a terribly long and exhausting night. If you'd gotten here when you were supposed to, you would know that." Worried she'd say something to Jack she'd definitely regret

BLUE RIDGE DANGER

later, she walked toward Carter, her lips pressed tight in aggravation.

Jack opened his mouth to say something, then apparently thought better of it as he just closed the trunk of his vehicle. Also with a little more force than necessary.

"Is he your boyfriend?" Carter asked quietly, motioning to Jack.

Rylie laughed at the odd question. "Jack? No. He's my cameraman and assistant. We're just friends."

"He doesn't think you're just friends." Carter watched Jack for a few seconds, his mind obviously traveling several miles in a short time. He shrugged, his expression returning to its stoic norm. "When he's ready, bring him to the office for his cabin key."

Carter turned and walked away. His abrupt departure left her feeling some kind of way. She'd never even gotten to the part where the killer had been Jack's brother. His observation reflected exactly what she wanted him to think. So, why did it bother her so much that he thought Jack was her boyfriend?

Jack appeared at her side the instant Carter left. "Tall, blond, and broody have a bear to wrestle or something?"

"He's a good man. And generous enough to share his land." She suspected it was way harder for him to do than he'd let on thus far. "So be nice. We need his cooperation."

Jack scoffed. "Yeah, I heard. A real hero. If he was so good at saving people, Darcy would still be alive. And Mason isn't dead."

She bristled at his comment. "What does Carter have to do with any of that?"

He turned to look at her, a dramatic expression of overplayed shock on his face. "You know he was there. He got himself shot and couldn't take out Mason like he should have."

"You wanted him to *kill* Mason?" This shocked Rylie.

Jack shrugged. "Mason's been evil since the day he came into this world. Someone needed to put him down before he killed again."

"Again?" Rylie asked. "He's killed other people?"

Jack walked back to the stack of equipment on the ground and started grabbing up bags and cases. "When he was nine. The files were sealed, though, because he was a kid. Jury decided it was an accident. That a nine-year-old didn't have the mental capacity to intentionally kill a toddler."

The level of nonchalance in his tone discon-certed her.

She tilted her head to the side, studying her cameraman, trying to decide if he was serious or not. "So, you blame Carter for Mason shooting him instead of the other way around?"

"Pretty much, yeah." Jack shrugged.

"That makes absolutely no sense." Rylie picked up a couple of bags and led him to the office. "Now look who's kept a few skeletons in their proverbial closet."

Jack frowned. "Those aren't my particular skele-tons. They all belong to my sociopathic brother."

What did he mean by *not my particular skele-tons*? She didn't have time to dissect the statement at the moment, but she did make a mental note to return to the conversation later.

"Hang out here. I'll grab the key to your cabin from Carter. When the others get here, we'll show them the dormitory. You and I get private spaces." Rylie set down the bags she'd carried and strolled over to the office door.

Pushing it open, she saw the inner door had been closed, and the key to cabin five sat on the welcome counter.

"I wonder what's got into his briefs." Rylie

grabbed the key and headed back to where Jack waited.

When she stepped outside, Rylie nearly collapsed in laughter. Jack lay flat on his back on the ground. Jay knelt on his chest, fist poised to strike like a cobra at its prey.

"This isn't funny!" Jack choked out from under the boy's weight. "Call off your mutt!"

"I got him, Miss Rylie! The guy who wrecked your car and killed the owl!" Jay looked so proud of himself, she hated to tell him the truth.

"He's not the guy, Jay. Let him up, please. He's my assistant." Rylie offered Jay a hand, pulling him to his feet as Jack tried to shove him off his chest.

"But he has the bag with the bow and arrow." Jay pointed at a large bag. "I'm sure I saw him last night too!"

"That's camera equipment, moron. Very expensive equipment you better not have broken! I wasn't even here last night! Idiot." A very angry Jack started scooping up all his stuff again. "Where am I taking this?" he demanded of Rylie.

She handed him the key. "That cabin right there."

Jay had growled when Jack called him an idiot,

taking a step forward, but Rylie placed a hand on his shoulder, stopping him.

"Lighten up, Jack. He's just a kid who had a very traumatic experience last night."

"Whatever. You got patience for everyone here but me, the one who's been by your side through everything." He stormed away as fast as his heavy load would allow.

"Yeah, okay. If you say so," she said quietly enough that no one would hear her.

"I'm sorry, Miss Rylie. I thought he wanted to hurt you." Jay looked so distraught, she wrapped an arm around him and gave him a hug. "I really thought I saw him last night."

"You did good, honey. Thank you for having my back."

He shrugged off the praise. "I'm going to go clean up the broken glass in the dining hall, and then I'll change the tire on Officer Marshall's truck."

"You know he's not a cop anymore. I'm sure you can call him Carter."

"Oh, hell no. He'd just get someone else up here to lock me up for being rude or something." Jay grunted. "He's a mean old cuss."

Rylie bit back laughter at the very old-fashioned phrase and pointed toward the dining hall. "How about I head to the kitchen and make us something to eat while you work? I'm starving. Again."

"I guess I could eat." Jay sauntered away, trying to look indifferent, but if she had to guess, he was actually happy to be here, and she had a solid feeling as to why. Two hot meals in twelve hours and a safe place to sleep could go a long way for the kid.

CHAPTER EIGHT

CARTER CAUGHT JAY'S TAKEDOWN OF JACK through the window of the camp office. He laughed so hard, he nearly fell out of his chair watching the scrawny teenager tackle the man. Jack went down hard, probably with a burst of cussing that would make a grown man blush.

Jack had rubbed Carter the wrong way immediately. His gut told him the guy had his eye on Rylie, who appeared to have absolutely no interest in him beyond work and friendship. She'd even laughed him off when Carter mentioned it.

He let out a huge yawn. The lack of sleep had begun to catch up with him.

"I need coffee." Carter stood up, grabbed a flannel shirt off the back of his chair, and pulled it on. The mornings had started coming in crisp. Sitting outside all night had definitely given him a chill. After a hot cup of java, he'd take an even hotter shower and maybe grab some shut-eye for a couple of hours.

The walk to the dining hall took him past the place where Rylie's trashed car still sat, waiting to be towed. The whole thing made very little sense. She hadn't been in town but a few hours. Unless someone had followed her to the campground from LA, but that seemed pretty far-fetched.

One thing he knew for sure, though. The dead owl was far too sophisticated to have been the work of young Jay Standish. The boy had anger problems and abandonment issues, but he didn't even know Rylie. He had gotten into his fair share of trouble, but Carter didn't see the boy as violent.

As he passed by his truck, he could see Jay had already jacked it up and taken off the slashed tire.

"Morning, Jay. You sleep okay?" Carter asked.

The boy grunted and shrugged. "I guess."

"I'm going to get some coffee."

Jay motioned toward the chow hall, a slight smile lifting the corners of his mouth. "Miss Rylie is making breakfast."

Jay went back to work on changing the tire, basically dismissing Carter. Clearly, the boy preferred *Miss Rylie* over him.

Carter knew he didn't have any pancake mix, yet as he entered the building, he definitely smelled pancake deliciousness. His mouth was watering by the time he reached the kitchen.

"Are you actually making pancakes?" he asked when he saw Rylie.

She looked up from the griddle lined with circles of batter. "I am. You hungry, Mr. Marshall?"

"Call me Carter."

She nodded. "Okay. Are you hungry, Carter Marshall?"

He frowned. "Just Carter."

Rylie grinned at him. "Are you hungry, *Just Carter*?"

Carter opened his mouth to retort but closed it when he saw the humor in her eyes. He relaxed a little in the wake of her infectious smile. "Famished. It's almost like we didn't eat last night." His stomach let out a loud growl, punctuating his statement. "But I know I didn't have any pancake mix. How did you get down the mountain to get some?"

She laughed, her green eyes lighting up. "I didn't. You have flour, sugar, salt, eggs, and milk. I just mixed them all up."

Of course she did. Apparently, he'd been way off base with the cereal comment the day before. "I guess you're a pretty good cook?"

"She's one of the best." Jack stood in the open back door. "Aren't you, Rylie?"

The hairs on the back of Carter's neck bristled, warning him to watch out for the other man.

Rylie grinned at him. "I do okay."

"Is there something you need, man?" Carter asked, hoping he didn't sound as annoyed as Jack made him feel.

"I found everything I needed, thanks." Jack narrowed his eyes at Carter.

Ignoring the other man's glare, Carter grabbed a mug and poured a cup of the coffee Rylie had already brewed. It felt kind of nice walking into a kitchen and not being the one having to do all the cooking.

The hot caffeine-filled liquid gave him the boost he needed almost immediately, altering his original plan of taking a shower and a nap. "As soon as Jay finishes changing my tire, I'm going to drive him home and grab some supplies. When do your cast members arrive?"

Just asking the question made him feel like a total sellout.

You need the money. That's all. And maybe a little help with the guilt.

The guilt had been a heavy load to carry. When he'd offered up his property, it had been a way to assuage that feeling. It hadn't helped yet, but he held out hope despite the feeling that he'd sold his soul to the devil for a fat check that would go a long way with his campground survival school.

"Tomorrow morning." Rylie used a wide spatula to turn all the pancakes. She grabbed a couple plates as the food finished cooking, and then she plated them. "Jack and I will make a plan and set up the interview and challenge areas, and then we'll wire the campsites with cameras for the twenty-four-hour recording."

"After we eat, let's walk the property, Rylie. Get a feel for things," Jack said. "Marty is gonna have the buses up here at 8:00 a.m. sharp."

He talked right past Carter as though he wasn't there.

Rylie handed them each a plate of pancakes. "The syrup's on the counter over there." She gave a little laugh. "What's left of it after last night's redecorating anyway."

Jack looked like he wanted to interject but didn't get the chance.

"Wow! It smells great in here! I'm starving!" Jay burst into the room in a flurry of excitement that dimmed the second he saw Carter.

"Give me five minutes, and I'll have a stack of flapjacks taller than your head."

"Thanks," he mumbled, studying the floor tiles.

"You need to get the kid out of here before we start filming." Jack pushed in beside Rylie. "It's a violation of... of something, I'm sure. Besides, we've got things to do. You can't be spending all morning cooking for strangers."

"Back off, Jack." Rylie stepped closer to the griddle and started flipping pancakes. "We are all hungry, including you." She glanced pointedly at Jack's now-empty plate.

The man really got on Carter's nerves. "Once Jay has a chance to eat, I'm taking him home and going on a supply run for the week. You'll have all the time you need then to get things set up."

Rylie plated a large stack of pancakes and handed the dish to Jay. The way the boy's entire face lit up only for her irritated Carter. "Thank you so much, Miss Rylie."

Carter turned his attention to his own food, making quick work of it. As he rinsed the plate, Jack and Rylie chatted about the best place for campfire meetings and challenges.

"Does anyone else smell that?" Jay asked around a huge bite of food.

"Smell what?" Rylie asked.

"Smoke. It smells like something burning." He jumped up from the stool he'd been perched on and ran to the front of the dining room. "Fire! There's a cabin on fire!"

"What?" Carter let go of the plate he held. As it hit the stainless steel sink with a crash, he took off after Jay.

"It better not be mine!" Jack yelled, following them. "All my gear is in there!"

As Carter made it out the door of the dining hall, large orange flames licked at the sky from one of the empty cabins.

"Holy hell!" Carter sped up, racing toward the burning cabin. Just as he got close enough to feel the heat, the roof collapsed, sending up a shower of sparks that rained down all around him. Thankfully, the cabin sat far away from the others. A quick assessment proved that none of the sparks had set off a chain-reaction fire.

The closest water source was a hose at the back of the dining hall building. They'd never be able to save the structure. Instead, he stood there, watching one small piece of his dream turn to ash.

Jay, Jack, and Rylie stood around him, also watching.

"You want me to get a hose and try to put it out?" Jay asked, his tough exterior melting away with the burning cabin. Something resembling fear seemed to take its place.

"Hmpf. The building is a goner. Can't save it now." Jack clapped Carter on the shoulder, squeezing a touch harder than he needed to. "Better get it cleaned up ASAP so your contract doesn't void."

Jay squared his shoulders and glared at Jack, the tough veneer back in place. "Why are you such a jerk?"

"Just stating the facts, kid. If that makes me a jerk, I can own it. We have a job to do here, and Mr. Marshall has to do his part if he wants to get paid."

"Jack!" Rylie snapped. "Enough already. Carter knows the terms. The damn thing just burned down. Give him a minute. We don't even know *why* it caught fire. Besides, it has no bearing on filming the show."

Jack laughed without humor. "Have you looked around? This place is a dump. I can't believe this is the paradise you've chosen to run the show. Darcy would be so disappointed." He gestured to the pile of still-burning rubble. "The cabin was old, and the wood dried out. Anything could have started it, and all these buildings are just as much of a run-down mess."

"Watch it, man." Carter stepped in close, using his height advantage to try to intimidate Jack. "I offered this place because I wanted to help out. I don't need you or your network traipsing around here when I could be running my school instead. And for all we know, *you* could have set the fire! Being fashionably late for breakfast and all."

Jack raised his fists in a fighting stance. "Why would I waste a good match on anything in this dump!"

Carter growled. "You just can't appreciate anything not constructed in concrete! Go back to the city, bougie boy!"

Rylie elbowed her way in between them. Placing one hand on his chest and the other on Jack's, she physically pushed them apart. "You both need to just stop already." She turned to Carter. "Bougie boy? Really?" Then to Jack. "Insensitive and rude much? Don't make me pull rank on you."

"Look at him!" Carter waved a hand in Jack's

direction. "Dress pants and a button-down shirt with church shoes! What is with you city people and ridiculous shoes?"

"Better than looking like a caveman who just learned to chew with his mouth closed!" Jack shot back.

Carter glared at Jack, who just sneered at him in response.

Rylie pushed Jack backward lightly, creating a larger gap between them. "If we're done comparing penis sizes, both of you need to grow up and start acting like adults. We have bigger problems than who can flex better."

"The two of you are worse than the kids at school. I thought adults knew better." Jay huffed and walked away toward the dining hall.

Despite how hard he tried not to, Carter had kind of started to like the kid.

"He's got a real attitude problem." Jack shook his head. "Must be something to do with living in the middle of nowhere." He sneered at Carter. "He could be your kid with his same winning personality."

"Jack." Rylie's voice held a light warning. "Why don't you go change and grab your gear. We have a lot of work to do."

Carter watched Jack's expression carefully as he turned his attention back to Rylie.

"That's how it is now, Rylie? Or should I say *boss*?" His tone was very annoyed as he stared her down.

The way she held her stance and countered Jack's hard stare impressed him. Carter almost smiled at the challenge in her eyes.

"I know you can appreciate the tight schedule we have. Not to mention, a little empathy might be nice over the loss of one of the buildings on Mr. Marshall's property." Her voice stayed steady as she continued to challenge her assistant's behavior.

Finally, Jack responded. "I need to get the gear unpacked and start making a plan for filming. I'll catch up with you in about thirty minutes." He turned and strode away, shoulders rigid.

"I hate to break it to you, but that guy is a real jerk." Carter slowly shook his head. "He better watch his step around Staunton. Local folks won't take kindly to his city attitude."

Rylie looked over at him. "Darcy was his boss too. This has been hard on him since the man—since he knew the killer."

Carter held his hands up in mock surrender.

"You two do what you gotta do. I'm outta here for now."

He strode off toward his truck, the need for a nap long gone after the adrenaline rush of the fire and face-off with Jack. Once he got Jay home and picked up supplies, he'd deal with the burnt-out skeleton of a building smoldering against the backdrop of the Blue Ridge Mountains.

Too many fires were burning on his mountain at once. He needed a little distance from them all.

CHAPTER NINE

THE SMELL OF THE SMOLDERING FIRE BURNED her lungs as they walked past the remains of the cabin.

"Do you smell gas?" She stopped walking and scanned the charred remains of the structure. "This pile has a distinct odor of gasoline."

Jack frowned, making a big production of sniffing the air. "Nope. I just smell a giant campfire. And a little bit of satisfaction that our host has to clean it up."

Rylie planted her hands on her hips. "Now what exactly is that supposed to mean? Can't you see how hard it is for him to do this?"

"Do what?" Jack demanded. "Let us use his land? Maybe if he would have done his job and

121

stopped Mason from killing Darcy, our family property wouldn't have become a crime scene, and we wouldn't have had to change locations. Besides, he's being paid a lot of money."

"Wow, Jack. I can't even with you right now." She stormed away.

Jack followed, grabbing her by the arm to keep her from leaving. She yanked free but stopped walking.

"Look, I'm sorry. It's just such a sore spot still. Mason's in prison, probably for life. Don't get me wrong, that's where he should be. Still, my parents are a mess over the whole thing. And, well, so am I." He looked down at the ground as he shoved his hands into his pockets. "I'll try harder not to be such a jerk, okay?"

He looked so forlorn; she couldn't not forgive him. At least for the sake of the show. They were stuck here for the next few weeks. Darcy had been his brother's fiancée *and* his boss. Rylie couldn't begin to imagine what his family had been going through. Sometimes she forgot the weight Jack had to be carrying over Mason.

Rylie had never met Jack's brother. She'd showed up late that day due to car trouble, and the hostages were already being held in the farmhouse. Mason had been removed so swiftly from the scene once he'd been in custody, she never saw him. All Jack had ever said about Mason was that they were never very close.

Avoiding the image of Darcy's killer had probably been for the best. Since he'd pled guilty to the charges, there were no court proceedings. The only picture she'd seen in the paper showed long, unkempt hair falling over his face. Jack said his brother had never had social media, so there wasn't anything the gossip sites could post. Mason had managed to live completely out of the digital age, and Darcy had never once introduced him to anyone at work. Maybe she knew he wasn't quite right? No matter the reason, it kept the enemy of her nightmares a faceless one, and for that she was extremely grateful.

Rylie offered a small smile. "Okay. But I'm holding you to it. We have too much to do for the show for you to be nursing a grudge." She pointed at a large grassy area. "I think we'll set up the campfire meets over there. We need logs or rocks to sit on and plenty of wood ready to go. Also, a fire ring made of rocks. Keep it as rustic as possible."

Jack made some notes on the tablet. "Got it. I'll

put the crew to work first thing when they get here. How about the challenges?"

"There's an amazing waterfall area I want to show you. I want to work it into at least a couple shoots." Rylie headed toward her little treasure find from the night before. Jack followed, grumbling to himself.

THEY SPENT the next several hours mapping things out and setting up as much as they could without any other crew. By early afternoon, Carter had been gone a long time. Rylie found herself straining to hear the sound of his truck returning.

When she finally did hear the engine roaring, it was close to three in the afternoon. Jack had gone into his cabin to work on a layout for his cameras at the campsites for the two teams.

Rylie had settled herself on a large tree stump. She had her laptop with her, and she reviewed contestant files as she tried to divide them into two comparable teams, following Darcy's original plans as closely as she could. Things were going to be very interesting, as not one of the contestants had any survival skills whatsoever. They had two office managers, a banker, a broker off Wall Street, a dancer, and two teachers among the group. Not to mention her personal favorite, a fortune teller from a traveling carnival.

Carter's truck came into view surrounded by a cloud of dust. Her heart skipped an unexpected beat at the sight of him. The grumpy ex-cop turned survival instructor had a certain appeal. She found herself wondering what kinds of things he could teach *her*.

Embarrassment flooded through her at some of the thoughts trying to sneak into the creative part of her brain.

She stood up and set her computer down. She remained professional even as the most perfect-fitting pair of faded jeans she'd ever seen became visible as Carter stepped down out of his truck.

She waved at him... or maybe she fanned herself. Either way, it worked. "Everything go okay? You've been gone a long time."

Carter gave her an odd look. "I had several stops to make."

Darn it! She hadn't meant to say that.

"I meant, did everything go okay with Jay's dad? I worried he might have given you a hard time."

A lousy Hail Mary of a save, but at least she'd tried.

Carter nodded. "Everything went fine. His old man was passed out on the couch, so there was no confrontation. I had lunch with a couple of my brothers today and had a bunch of supplies to pick up. The network sent me funds to purchase some of the things y'all will need that I didn't already have. Your boss figured I'd know what to buy and where, I guess."

Suddenly annoyed, Rylie frowned. She didn't know the network had done that. She made a mental note to remind her bosses that she needed to be kept in the loop on every single detail.

"I'll help you unload." Hopefully Carter hadn't picked up on her irritation at not knowing about the supply money.

The back of his SUV was stacked top to bottom with food and other gear. Rylie reached up to the top of the load to grab a box from a local hardware store, but when she gave it a tug, it wouldn't move. She pulled harder, and it slid forward faster and way heavier than she'd expected.

"Rylie!" Carter yelled as he jumped in behind her and grabbed the box before it tumbled onto her head. As his arms reached around her to stop the cargo from falling, she felt every inch of him pressed against every inch of her. The heat erupting from the intimate contact sent such a zing through her system that Rylie gasped.

"You really could have been hurt," Carter said as he lifted the box up and over her. "This one is full of the cast-iron skillets and aluminum pots I didn't have enough of for the water and cooking challenges."

She bristled. No wonder it had been so ridiculously heavy. "Didn't anyone ever teach you that the heavy, dangerous stuff goes at the bottom? Not at the very top!"

"I didn't expect anyone else to unload the truck but me." His breath feathered her ear as he spoke, low and gruff, washing all her aggravation away at once. Did he feel the heat she did?

Rylie's ribs ached from her heart slamming against them. She couldn't be exactly sure if the adrenaline rush came from the near-death-by-cast-iron experience or the full-body contact with Carter, but she suspected it was the latter.

When she finally mustered up the courage to look him in the eye, Carter had an odd look on his face. Maybe he *had* felt the electricity sparking where they made physical contact. Or was he just worried about a lawsuit if she got hurt on his property?

"Do you want me to store this in the barn, or do you have somewhere else you'd like it to go?" he asked, sounding slightly shaken.

Her mind screamed, *Yes—he felt it too!* Her body, however, bellowed, *No!* as Carter put a considerable distance between them.

"The barn is fine. We can keep everything in there and only bring it out when we need it. The teams will each be given certain items, like the cookware, up front. But for now, we can use the barn to store and sort." Rylie heard herself rambling. She tried to stop, but her mouth seemed completely disconnected from her brain. "I mean, if it's okay with you?"

Carter nodded, not quite making eye contact. "It's fine. If you can grab those two bags right there." He pointed at some hefty tote bags. "Those have the ropes, the flints, and the knives in them. We can take it all at once."

Rylie pulled out the two bags, and they headed to the barn. Neither of them spoke. The tension became almost palpable.

"Hey! What are you two doing?" Jack's voice cut like a knife, slicing through the air between them and freeing them of whatever seemed to be manipulating the tension. He caught up with them as they reached the double barn doors. "I need to be the one to help you set up the sites."

"We were just stowing these items in here. No setting up yet." Rylie hoped she didn't sound as annoyed as she felt, but when she caught the look in Carter's eyes, she knew she did.

"We really need to get the survival gear sorted into the crates. I'll help you right now so it's done correctly." Jack moved in between Rylie and Carter. "I can take it from here, Marshall."

Without a word, Carter turned and handed Jack the box he carried. "You got it, dude. I'll be in the kitchen, putting food away." His eyes glinted with humor as he winked at Rylie.

The box was obviously far heavier than Jack had expected. The sudden weight caused him to stumble forward and grunt from the effort of making it look like he could carry it as effortlessly as Carter had.

"Thanks, man. We'll catch you later." Jack gasped the words, trying so hard to sound calm, cool, and collected.

Rylie snorted.

Although good-looking in his own right, Jack stood a good four inches shorter and several muscle sizes smaller than Carter. Rylie held back a grin as Jack worked overtime to keep his ego intact.

"You got that, buddy?" Carter asked, casually leaning against a stall stacked with canvas bags containing tents.

Ignoring Carter's taunt, Jack walked over to a workbench and dropped the box on top with a loud clatter. "Come on, Rylie. Let's get this stuff divided up for the meet and greet with the teams tomorrow."

"Okay. Fine." Rylie glanced back at Carter, but all she caught was a quick look at his back as he disappeared out the open doors. "I don't get why you're always so rude to Carter. You promised to not be a jerk anymore."

Rylie started unpacking the boxes and bags, spreading the items across the bench so she could see what they'd procured.

Jack gave a dramatic look of shock as he motioned to the box he'd finally unloaded onto the counter. "Me? I'm not rude at all. He did this on purpose."

"Did what? Gave you the box you demanded?" Rylie shrugged. "If you ask me, your ego got you exactly what you deserve. Carter is a very strong man."

"And what? I'm not?" he snapped.

This time she actually laughed. "Come on, Jack. You can't think you actually match his strength? You're not even the same height, not to mention anything else."

He scoffed. "You've got a point. No way I could stack up to a mountain man. He probably lifts boulders in the morning instead of going to the gym. Tears raw meat apart with his bare hands...."

She doubled over in laughter. "He's not a caveman!"

Jack turned to look at her, his expression serious. "You and I are a lot alike, Rylie. We could be so great together. A real power couple at the network, if you'd just give us a chance."

"There is no us." She stepped back, needing a lot of space between them.

Jack shrugged. "I don't see why not. We have similar goals. We'd make gorgeous kids and rock the red carpet every time one of our shows was nominated for an Emmy!"

He moved in so close, she felt trapped between him and the wall. Quickly sidestepping, she avoided his touch and put some more distance back between them.

"Unless, of course, you prefer men who grunt and pull ticks off their mates."

Rylie forced a smile. "I've told you before, Jack. I'm not interested in being in a relationship with anyone at the moment. I have to put my career first. This show, it *has* to be amazing. It's the only chance I have to make a name for myself in the business after what happened with Darcy. My livelihood and my job depend on it. Per the network. I don't have time for anything else right now."

Jack pouted. "I bet if tall, blond, and annoying wanted you, though, he wouldn't even have to ask. He could just grunt and maybe sling some poo at you like a monkey."

She couldn't help but laugh at the ridiculous image he had elicited. "Please just let me concentrate on the show while we're here. It's too important to me to let anything mess it up."

Jack exhaled dramatically. "Fiiiiine. But we'll revisit this conversation after you ace the ratings and win over the network."

Rylie couldn't even begin to dare to dream that way. All she wanted was to rebuild her reputation and maybe get a raise so she could have an apartment with a separate bedroom.

"There's nothing to revisit, Jack. We work well together. Don't mess it up with weird sexual advances."

"Fine. But I'm a persistent son of a bitch. I'll win you over eventually."

She sighed. "Let's just finish up here. I have a lot of work to do still."

Jack seemed to take the hint. They spent the next hour creating crates and discussing the plan for the show. Each team would get a cast-iron skillet, a flint, a pot with a lid, some rope, and a large knife. During their time on the show, the challenges would involve using those items to perform survival skills like starting a fire, building a small shelter, catching a fish and cooking it, and setting a snare.

Rylie felt good about the plan for the show. As long as there were no more fires or vandalism, she expected things to go smoothly.

"Do you have the cameras set up at the camp-sites?" she asked Jack as they finished up.

"Not yet, but I have them laid out on paper and am heading there after we finish up here." He double-checked the last crate. "This one is good to go."

"Why don't you head out, then. I'm going to check out the other equipment Carter has in here. I want to be sure he has fishing hooks and line." Rylie motioned around the barn. "I'm sure they're in here somewhere."

Jack looked reluctant to leave but nodded in agreement as he checked his watch. "I don't want it to get dark on me before I finish. I'll check in when I'm done."

"Perfect." She gave him a quick smile. "Thank you for being here and helping me. I'm sorry for being a little bristly earlier."

He shrugged. "No worries. I'm used to it."

Before she could retort, he turned and strode away.

Rylie began her tour of the barn, looking for the fishing gear Carter had mentioned during one of their phone calls. She had finally located the shelf where it was all stored when the lights suddenly went out. A second or two later, the doors slid shut, and she heard the sound of the locking mechanism clicking into place.

"Wait! No! I'm still in here!" Rylie moved as quickly as she dared through the pitch-black space to where she thought the doors were. Pounding on the wood, she continued to yell. "Carter! Let me out! Please! Come back! I'm still in here!"

Reaching into her pocket for her cell phone, she realized she'd dropped it somewhere in the large structure. It could be anywhere. She exhaled her frustration.

"Help!" she yelled once more, her face pressed against the wood. Whoever had closed the doors had to have heard her yelling. Why didn't they open them back up?

Her entire life, she had been afraid of the dark, and forget about small spaces. The barn, although large, had the same claustrophobic effect on her.

Rylie slid down the wall to the floor, resting her arms on her knees.

She had to find her phone so she could call for help. Carter wouldn't know to look for her, and Jack would probably assume she'd gone back to her cabin to look at scripts and things.

Rylie began to shake as fear rushed through her veins. She couldn't lose it now. Spending the night in a dark, scary barn couldn't happen.

The show's host would arrive in the morning. She needed to get ready for him and the contestants coming by bus a few hours later. There was no time to lose her mind. She had a show to do, and that began with getting out of the barn.

"Okay, Rylie. It's time to pull up your big girl panties and find your phone. There's nothing in here in the dark that wasn't in here in the light. You can do this."

Her pep talk did little to convince her. Too many

old fears were having their way with her at the moment.

She finally pulled herself to her feet as her eyes adjusted some to the dimness in the barn. Large shapes began to form. If she just followed the workbench they'd been using to the end and then retraced her steps from when she'd searched for the fishing gear, she should be okay.

"Stop being such a wuss. You've got this, girl." Saying the words out loud, hoping her own voice would make her feel brave, didn't work at all. Her hands still shook as adrenaline threatened to take her places in her head she hated going.

Using the wall as a guide, she made her way to the workbench. From there, she moved while slowly scuffing her feet along the floor in an effort to locate her missing cell. As she rounded the edge of a stall, Rylie paused to get her bearings again.

As she took a deep breath and prepared to continue on, something slammed into her forehead, sending her to the floor with its force.

The hit came so fast, Rylie barely made a sound as she crumpled. "Who... who's there?" she managed to murmur as warm liquid ran into her eyes and her vision began to grow dark.

CHAPTER TEN

Once he'd stowed the provisions in the dining hall, Carter went to his office to get some work done. His hope in offering his property to the show was to drive up business. Well, his secondary hope anyway. What he really hoped was that he'd be able to drop some of the guilt over losing a domestic violence victim even a rookie should have been able to save. He'd also really like to start sleeping again.

A loud clap of thunder caught his attention in a hurry. Carter glanced out the window to see the sky darkening in the west. Rolling black clouds moved at a surprisingly fast pace toward his mountain.

"Those look like hail clouds." Carter pulled out his cell phone and opened the local weather app. Sure enough, the first thing he saw was severe weather moving in and the instructions to find a safe place in case a tornado decided to form. Apparently, conditions were favorable for a twister to touch down.

A sharp bolt of lightning quickly followed by another clap of thunder really got his attention. He better check on Rylie and the doofus she had assisting her up here. It certainly wouldn't help his business if something happened to one or both of them. Especially not once word of the car and the owl got around. He didn't have a lot of faith in Peters's discretion.

The moment he stepped outside, the rain started. The unseasonably warm fall day had completely disappeared. Large, icy-cold drops of rain slammed into his body. The late-October weather could make for some chilly evenings on the mountain. Add in wind and rain, and one could develop hypothermia pretty quickly.

Carter pulled up the collar of his flannel and yanked his baseball hat lower over his brow. By the time he reached Rylie's cabin, the hail had begun. Ice rocks the size of dimes and quarters pummeled him as he banged on the door.

"Rylie! Open up!"

No response. Maybe she'd decided to take a nap.

Some people could sleep through anything. "I really hope she's not out on the property somewhere." Carter ran to the back of the cabin and peered in through the window, trying to see if maybe Rylie was in the bathroom.

The cabin looked empty. The hail continued. Every point of contact felt like a golf ball slamming into him.

He went back around front, calling for her in the direction of the campsites. "Rylie!"

Jack's cabin door flew open, worry all over his face. "Isn't she in her cabin?"

"If she is, she's ignoring me and the storm!" Carter yelled over the ever-rising winds and pounding rain.

The other man came outside, wearing only a T-shirt and jeans with no shoes, shocking Carter as he raced over to the next structure to pound on the door. "Rylie! You in there? Come on! Open the door!"

When it became obvious to him that she wasn't in there, Jack looked panicked. "We have to find her! She'll never survive this out there!"

Although he was quite certain Rylie was far stronger than Jack insinuated, he wasn't taking any chances. Carter had already begun heading to the campsites. "I'm ten steps ahead of ya, buddy!"

There was absolutely no way another woman would be hurt on his watch.

Without waiting for the other man, Carter ran as fast as the weather would permit. With each step, his boots slipped on wet leaves and mud, but he pushed through the driving rain, hail, and winds, frantically determined.

It wouldn't be good for his business if Rylie died out there in the storm.

At least, that was how he justified his insane need to find her safe and sound.

His head was on board, but his heart and soul would never survive another loss of an innocent person. Especially not here on his land. Definitely not Rylie Christianson.

"Rylie! Rylie, where are you?" His words were gobbled up by the raging storm. There was no way she'd ever hear him when he could barely hear himself!

Within a flash of lightning, he caught sight of the barn. There was a chance she could be inside, riding out the storm. He had to check. With any luck, she'd be dry and safe and would give him a lecture on running around in nasty storms like a crazy man.

Changing directions, Carter ran straight to the closed double doors of the barn. Somehow a large branch had jammed into the slide mechanism for opening the doors. Fighting against the strong wind gusts yet again, he yanked at the branch, trying to work it free. The hail had finally stopped, but the wind-whipped downpour still continuously slapped him in the face. The horrific conditions combined with his drenched clothes made it extremely difficult to manipulate the jammed wood. He'd almost given up when the branch finally came free. The force of it snapping loose sent him to the muddy ground.

Carter crashed into the mud and storm debris. The pain of landing on a rock with his right kneecap nearly caused him to black out. Fireworks of agony shot through his entire body as the muscles, ligaments, and tendons of the injured joint refused to cooperate with his brain and let him get back on his feet. The nerves screamed at him with every movement. He half crawled, half dragged himself to the doors and pushed them open, making a space just wide enough to force himself through.

Wind and rain followed him until he made it several feet into the darkness. Flopping over on his back, Carter lay there, steadying his breathing and taking stock. The only injury he was sure of—his knee—hurt like hell, but everything else felt okay.

He was in one piece anyway.

Digging in his jeans pocket, Carter found his cell phone. Thank God it hadn't been lost in the storm or broken when he'd hit the ground.

The flashlight function lit up the space pretty well. He raised himself into a seated position to assess his injury. As he poked and prodded his very painful knee, the storm continued to rage outside.

He had to get up and keep looking for Rylie. After using a support post to pull himself up to standing, Carter tentatively tested his injured leg. Streaks of white-hot pain shot straight to his core. "Damn it!"

Resting his weight on the post, he used the phone light to scan the barn. There had to be something he could use to help him walk. As he moved the light meticulously over every inch of the barn, he gasped. About twenty feet from where he was propped, Rylie lay on the floor. A small, dark puddle had formed next to her head. Even without the benefit of full illumination, he could tell it was blood.

"Rylie!" His voice echoed throughout the building. "Rylie! Wake up!"

She didn't respond at all. Not with a grunt or a groan. No movement either, and honestly, he couldn't even tell if she was breathing.

Ignoring the agony he experienced with every

step, Carter limped his way over to the motionless woman. He lowered himself to the floor beside her as carefully as he could, then felt for a pulse in her wrist. Carter exhaled sharply when he finally located one. The light thumping against his fingertips was far steadier than he'd expected it to be.

As he sat there, trying to figure out the best plan of action, Jack suddenly burst through the barn doors on a heavy gust of wind.

"Holy hell! This storm is wild!" Jack pulled the doors closed before acknowledging Carter. "Does this happen a lot up here?"

"Please find the light switch to the left of the door and turn on the lights," Carter requested, ignoring Jack's question.

A few seconds later, the barn was flooded in fluorescent light.

"Oh my God, is that *Rylie*?" Jack sprinted over to them and dropped to the floor on the opposite side of the unconscious woman.

"Is she dead?" he asked, pointing at the puddle of blood.

"No," Carter said. "But she won't wake up, so the head injury could be even worse than it looks."

He still had his hand on her wrist, monitoring Rylie's pulse. As long as it stayed steady, they had a little time. The storm still raged but with a bit less force. With any luck it would soon be over.

"We need to get her to the hospital!" Jack jumped up and reached for Rylie.

"No! Don't move her!" Carter pushed the other man's chest with his palms.

Jack grunted as he toppled backward and landed with a thump on his hind end. "What did ya go and do that for?"

"She could have a spinal injury! We don't know how she got here!" Carter practically growled at Jack. "What if she fell? Hit her head and twisted her neck? Any movement could leave her paralyzed for life."

Jack looked shocked. "I didn't think of that."

"You didn't think of that?" Rylie repeated in a raspy voice. "So, I could have ended up in a damn wheelchair and eating through a tube so you could play hero?"

Jack laughed. "And now we know she's okay."

Relief flooded through Carter with a force equal to that of the storm.

"Rylie, what happened?" He placed a gentle hand on her shoulder when she tried to sit up. "Did you fall?"

"My head hurts." She reached up to probe the

wound on her scalp, but Carter wrapped his large hand around her smaller one to stop her from touching it just in case.

Jack repeated Carter's question. "Did you fall or what?"

"No! I didn't fall. Someone hit me on the head." Rylie tried once more to sit up, but Carter stopped her again.

"Someone hit you on the head?" Carter immediately scanned the area, paying attention to every detail of every shadow.

"Are you sure you didn't just trip or something?" Jack asked.

The man was even more of a jackass than Carter had thought.

This time she ignored his desire for her to stay still and sat straight up. "Someone. Hit. Me. Over. The. Head. How many times do I have to say it? I didn't trip. I didn't fall. The same someone, or maybe an accomplice, closed the barn doors and locked them."

"That means they are still in here, right?" Jack sounded a little scared.

She shrugged. "Or they climbed out that window in the back. The storm came in so fast and so dark, I couldn't see anything at all for a minute."

Carter's mind flashed back to the damage to her rental car and the poor dead owl. He gave her hand a gentle squeeze. "I'm starting to think you really made someone very angry. And that you brought an angry psycho to my peaceful campground."

Rylie wiped away a tear. "I'm starting to think that too."

Jack paced around in the barn with no regard for Rylie or Carter as he mumbled to himself about stupid country people.

If he could have stood up, Carter might have shown him just how "country" he could be.

"Don't worry, we'll figure this out." Carter, still holding her hand, gave it another light squeeze. "In the meantime, I'm not sure you should be out on the property alone."

The roar of the wind had died down considerably. They'd probably be able to get out of there soon. Provided Carter's knee would let him walk. He flexed it a little, trying not to whimper when the same white-hot bolt of pain shot up his leg.

"Please believe me! I have no idea what's going on. I don't have a single enemy. I hardly even have friends. I work so much." Rylie sounded so sincere and concerned, Carter couldn't help but believe her.

Jack stayed surprisingly quiet, which was enough

to draw Carter's attention and create a few questions that needed addressing at some point.

"Let me take a look at your head." Carter shone the flashlight on his phone on Rylie's injury. "There's a lot of blood, but it looks to be superficial. Head injuries always bleed a lot because of all the blood vessels in the scalp."

Rylie placed her hand on his arm. "I swear someone hit me. And I double swear I don't know who or why."

The earnest plea in her eyes told him she was telling the truth. She really had no idea who was doing these things to her.

"I believe you." He glanced over at Jack. "You got any ideas? Like maybe it's been you all along?"

Jack glared at Carter. "Me? I would never hurt Rylie!"

"Relax, man. I meant maybe you're the target. All the same people who knew Rylie would be here also knew you would be here with her."

"Oh. Sorry." Jack's glare turned into a frown. "I guess I jumped the gun there."

"Ya think?" Rylie rolled her eyes, her irritation apparent.

Carter kept one eye on Jack while he talked to Rylie. The man set off his cop Spidey senses with every breath he took. "What about the cast? Anyone apply to be on the show and get turned down?"

"Hundreds of people," Jack said.

"Anyone especially angry about not making the cut?" Carter asked.

"There was some hate mail," Rylie said. "Actual letters as well as some emails. Nothing that made me think my life would really be in danger, though."

Jack strolled over to the open doors and looked out. "Looks like the worst of the storm has passed. Should we get out of here in case the guy is still around?"

His apprehension seemed almost palpable as he strode back to where Carter and Rylie still sat. He reached out. "Come on. I'll help you up, Rylie."

Carter knew his knee was still messed up without even trying to stand again. He waited until Jack had Rylie on her feet before choking back his ego. "Hey, can you give me a hand too? I banged up my leg pretty bad in the storm."

Jack looked reluctant to let go of Rylie, but she nodded. The man was obviously nursing a serious crush on her, but she didn't seem to notice.

"I'm good, Jack." Rylie leaned against the support post, turning her attention to Carter. "Can you walk if we can get you to your feet?"

"I just need to get up." Carter accepted Jack's outstretched hand and used it to pull himself up.

His knee screamed with pain, but he managed to stay upright. At least it let him put a little pressure on it finally. Pointing toward a rack near the doors, he asked, "Hey, Jack, can you grab me one of the kayak oars over there on the wall?"

"Fine." He muttered something else under his breath, but Carter couldn't make it out.

"Here." Rylie shifted to her right. "Use the post to hold on to."

Carter leaned on the post. "I'm sorry."

"For what?" She looked at him, confused.

"You've been here twenty-four hours, and—" He waved a hand in front of them. "—this isn't what you signed up for. I promised you three weeks for producing your show, not being stalked by who knows who or what."

"Here." Jack shoved the oar at him. "Come on, Rylie. Put your arm around me and let me support you."

"You should probably help Carter. He's really injured. I'm fine." Rylie tried to duck out of his reach, but Jack was faster, wrapping an arm around her waist.

"He's fine. You're the one with the head injury."

Jack started leading her toward the door. Rylie gave up and let him.

She probably had one hell of a headache.

Carter tucked the oar under his arm and began limping after them. As they emerged from the barn, the wind still churned some, but the rain had stopped. The dark clouds had moved off to the north, lightening the sky enough that they could see their way back to the main area.

Watching the ground to avoid anything that might trip him up again, Carter limped along.

At least he didn't seem to have a fracture or anything. He could put some pressure on it and bend it farther the more steps he took.

As he trailed behind Jack and Rylie, Carter kept an eye on the cameraman. Something about Jack just didn't sit right with him.

As they reached the cabins, Jack led Rylie to hers. Carter spotted a huge old oak tree that had been uprooted and stretched across the road where it met the parking area. Just what he did not need at the moment.

"How are you feeling? Should we try to get EMS up here? I've got to call this in anyway." He'd somehow have to clear some of the tree to get them in, but he'd do it if Rylie needed it.

She shook her head. "No. I'm going to put some ice on it and maybe take a shower later to get the blood out of my hair, but I think I'm fine."

"Be careful you don't open the wound again if it's scabbed over. If you start to feel nauseous or dizzy, tell me, and we'll get you checked out."

"Don't worry, Marshall. I'll take care of her." The look Jack gave him over Rylie's shoulder was as smug as any he'd seen before.

Nope. He definitely didn't like or trust the man. Unfortunately, Rylie seemed to, and they did work together, so he had no say in what they did with each other, even if he hated the idea of such a jerk sitting in Rylie's cabin with her.

Why he hated it was another thing he might need to examine later.

Along with why he thought Jack was a jerk with an agenda.

Maybe not in that exact order, though.

"Okay, then. Just call if you need anything. The kitchen is fully stocked now, so help yourself to anything you want. I'll see y'all in the morning. I'm going to let the police department know someone may have attacked Rylie. I'll give them your number so they can reach you."

Without waiting for a reply, Carter hobbled his

way past Jack and Rylie and let himself into his cabin. After leaving the oar propped against the outside of the building, he was able to walk carefully around the living area without support. The day had turned out nothing like he'd expected it to, and his entire body screamed for a hot shower, a beer, and his bed.

He grabbed his laptop off the tiny table in the main room and set it on his bed for after his shower. The tiny dorm-sized fridge by his bed held two things—bottled water and beer. He took out one of each and set the water on top of the fridge. He popped the top on the beer and took a long swig, letting the ice-cold liquid coat his insides and offer a balm to the pain in his knee.

Giving up the idea of a shower, Carter stripped out of his wet clothes and dropped onto the bed in just his boxer briefs. Maybe he'd just take a nap instead and deal with everything else in an hour or two. Honestly, it could all wait until morning.

CHAPTER ELEVEN

RYLIE SMACKED THE SMALL WINDUP ALARM clock on her nightstand. It fell to the floor with a sad clang, as though it had sounded its last alarm ever. Why couldn't she be one of those normal people who could wake up to pretty digital alarms on her phone? The kind that didn't start her off angry every day.

Her head ached, and her eyes begged to stay closed. The events of the previous day flooded back, right up to the point where Jack refused to leave her cabin, and she had to basically push him out the door. Carter, on the other hand, had been as protective and caring as he had that day back in high school.

At the moment, all her focus had to switch to the show and not Jack's uncomfortable presence or

Carter's amazingly strong arms she'd dreamed about supporting her back to her cabin the day before instead of her cameraman.

"Ugh! Focus, girl! Today's a big day. Your cast is coming, and you've got to start rolling cameras in twenty-four hours." Rylie continued her personal pep talk as she stepped into the tiny bathroom with its minuscule shower stall. Although grateful to not have to trek to the community bathhouse, the squeeze was tight as she carefully washed her long hair with the chilly well water.

As Rylie dried herself with one of the towels from the shelf over the toilet, her phone chimed with an incoming text message.

She wrapped the towel around her hair as she walked to the tiny table where she'd left her phone and then picked it up. Disappointment seeped in a tiny bit when she saw Jack's name on the screen. She'd kinda hoped Carter was texting to check on her.

Jack: Hey, how you doing this morning?

Rylie: Got a headache, but nothing some ibuprofen can't help with.

> Jack: Marshall's got some younger guy helping him cut up the downed tree. Maybe a brother?

> Rylie: Oh, good. You should help. Get it done faster so the bus can get up here.

> Jack: You want to go into town and get some breakfast and maybe find a real coffee place? Not sure I can stomach grocery store swill again, and they cleared enough of the tree to get out of here.

He just completely ignored her suggestion for helping the men remove the fallen tree. She pursed her lips in slight annoyance.

> Rylie: I've got way too much to do before the cast members get here. Why don't you stick around and help the guys with the tree instead?

Several seconds passed before those three dots reappeared, indicating Jack typing a response.

> Jack: I'll be back as soon as I can.

Rylie huffed. He'd ignored her *twice*.

Honestly, she'd expected Jack to hover all day

after her injury the night before. His choosing to leave *and* not help the guys surprised her.

She shivered at the memory of being locked in a dark building with some unknown psychopath.

At least nothing else had happened to her.

Rylie set her phone down, then dug out a pair of jeans and a sweatshirt with the network's logo on it. After tying her wet hair into a loose, messy bun, she sat down with her laptop and the files she'd brought with her. She'd formed two teams from the twelve cast members, and those six were divided into three males and three females. Well, almost. They'd had one nonbinary applicant. They agreed to work on whichever team she needed them to be on as long as they could participate. Rylie loved everything about their application and video and just had to have them on the show. Darcy had agreed.

Kent Patterson, her boss, had been concerned about the "sex thing"—aka mixing men and women on the same team—but Darcy had assured him that it wasn't going to be an issue, and Rylie had maintained that stance. He also had no idea what nonbinary meant, as he was nearly seventy years old and apparently existed in a technology-free box when not at work. Rylie smiled as she remembered the lesson on equity and workplace sensitivity she'd given him.

Kent had looked so confused by the time she'd explained the legal side of harassment and prejudice that she'd literally had to draw him a flowchart of "good" and "bad" points he had to know.

After one last look over everything, she felt convinced her teams were well balanced, based on the information provided by each applicant. She had people with little to no outdoor/survival-type experience who also really wanted to learn the skills. To create the competition the show's atmosphere needed, there were going to be challenges for small prizes throughout the duration as well as a grand prize for the winning team.

Glancing at her sad little alarm clock still lying awkwardly on the floor, Rylie was shocked to see she'd been deep in her work for over two hours. Her rumbling belly reinforced it, though. What was taking Jack so long?

After slipping her boots on, Rylie wandered out of her cabin and over to the dining hall. She only had about ninety minutes until the cast bus arrived, and she needed to eat something. If Jack showed up with food later, she could just eat it for her lunch.

The smell of deliciousness greeted her as she pulled the door open. Letting her nose lead the way, Rylie wound up in the kitchen, watching Carter making eggs—again. She chuckled. That man and his eggs....

His phone played some old '70s rock music as he sang along.

"You really don't eat too much variety, do you?"

Carter jumped, flinging the spatula he held across the room, barely missing her head. "Do you make a habit of sneaking up on people?"

Rylie laughed as she sidestepped the projectile. "Do you always throw utensils at people when they enter a room?"

Carter grabbed a clean spatula and went back to cooking. "I don't recommend ever sneaking up on a cop. Even an ex-cop. More often than not, it's not going to go well. What if I'd had a gun in my hand instead of a spatula?"

Rylie laughed. "Your gun would be hot steel instead of cold steel?"

For a moment she thought he would lose his temper. Instead, Carter laughed as well. "Yeah, okay. Seriously, though, it's never a good idea to sneak up on a cop. Even when he's no longer on the actual payroll."

"Duly noted. But you still haven't answered my question. You eat mostly eggs?"

Carter shrugged. "Like I told you yesterday, it's easy and does the job of making me not hungry."

She sighed. "It's so boring, though. I definitely need a little variety in all aspects of my life. And I feel like most of our conversations have revolved around food or vandalism. Have you noticed that?" Rylie rested a hand on one hip and leaned the other hip against the counter, waiting for him to reply.

Carter flipped the eggs he was frying. He then turned over the two sausage patties she hadn't noticed he had cooking. He set the utensil down and grabbed two English muffins, pulled them apart, and set them on the hot griddle.

"Eggs have variety. The other day we had omelets. Today I'm making sandwiches. And I added sausage." He plated them up and handed her one. "See? Variety."

His seriousness about it made her laugh again. "I'm thinking you don't actually get out too much, do you?"

He looked offended. "So? I like where I live. There are trees and animals and no neighbors."

"Whoa! It wasn't an insult. Sorry if I hit a nerve." Rylie took a bite of her sandwich and let out a little moan. "Boring or not, you're a complete whiz with eggs."

"Where's your boyfriend?" Carter asked, casually, taking a bite of his own sandwich.

"I told you, he's not my boyfriend. He went into town for some breakfast. Honestly, I expected him to be back by now. The buses with the cast and crew are due here in less than an hour. Also, I have no idea what happened to our host. He's thirty minutes late." Rylie grabbed a bottle of water from a package on the counter and took a long sip.

No sooner had the words left her mouth than she heard Jack's voice. "Rylie! You in here?"

He sounded irritated.

"If we stay quiet, maybe he won't find us," she whispered, holding a finger to her lips.

"Not likely. He's a bloodhound when it comes to you." The twitch of his lips looked almost like a smile trying to break through.

"Back here, man," Carter called out. "You want an egg sandwich?" he asked Jack as he entered the kitchen.

Jack scowled at the last bite of her sandwich. "I thought you had too much to do to eat."

"I never said that. I do have a lot to do, but I was also hungry. I just didn't want to leave the mountain on such a crazy day." Rylie stepped up to the sink and washed her hands. "You were gone a long time.

The buses will be here soon. You need to get your camera ready to film the arrivals of the contestants. The host should be here soon also."

"Will do. Let's talk before everyone arrives. I'll meet you out front with my gear in five?" Jack gave Carter a nod and sauntered off.

Rylie watched him leave, slightly amused. "Jack is always a little odd, but the past twenty-four hours or so have been kind of out of character even for him. I think you intimidate him."

Carter grabbed a tool and began scraping the grill. "I intimidate him? That's kinda funny, you know. I have absolutely no interest in him at all. Or the show. Just the check from your network. He can stop trying to compete or show his dominance or whatever. I'm not interested in engaging him."

"The two of you have some sort of crazy competition going on, and I just don't understand it." Rylie turned to leave. "If you'll excuse me, I need to go get ready to greet my staff and contestants."

CHAPTER TWELVE

CARTER WATCHED RYLIE WALK AWAY, UNABLE TO stop until she was out of sight. She was an ambiguity he just couldn't wrap his head around. He resented having strangers on his land, moving things around and just disturbing his peace. But for some reason, if it were just Rylie, he'd be okay with it. She was feisty yet sweet. Determined and had no inclination to put up with his dour attitude. He kind of liked that about her. Most people he knew just avoided him now. His brothers still treated him like an injured kitten. But Rylie? Her no-nonsense ways apparently had no time for his giant pity party.

Half an hour or so later, he heard the sounds of dueling engines making their way up the mountain road to the campground. Those had to be the buses

Rylie was waiting for. Earlier that morning, three dudes had arrived in a van and unloaded some electronics. He'd offered them the dining hall to set up shop if they needed to. The rest of the crew and the cast would be in those buses.

Carter had his table saw out and was working on covering the broken window with plywood until he could get the glass repaired. The tarp he'd nailed over it the day before was shredded in the storm. As he nailed up one section of wood, the first bus came into view.

The network had sprung for the fancy tour buses. The kind with the bathrooms and on-board movies. Carter had taken one of them to Washington, DC, for a middle school field trip. As a twelve-year-old kid, the cushy seats made him feel like royalty. Until he'd been forced to use the bathroom—something he never wanted to experience ever again.

Hopefully conditions had improved in the past fifteen or so years.

The first bus pulled to a stop where Rylie's rental car had been parked until a tow company hauled it away the night before. A handful of men and women exited the bus and began unloading recording equipment and suitcases from the cargo hold. He'd definitely expected the crew to be substantially larger.

As he hammered at a nail in the plywood, the second bus crested the hill to the campground, parking about twenty feet from its partner. No one exited the second bus, piquing his curiosity.

Rylie appeared a few moments later, exiting her cabin wearing a pair of jeans that looked like they'd been sewn together just for her, a soft black fitted sweater, and black military-style boots. She'd pulled her long chestnut hair into a ponytail and had a red-and-black plaid flannel shirt tied around her waist. He liked the jeans look way more than the tight dress and high heels. She headed to the second bus, followed closely by Jack carrying a camera and mic system. As they strode toward their destination, Rylie's hands moved animatedly as she gave Jack instructions.

When they reached the bus, Jack set up his camera stand as Rylie entered the vehicle. A minute or so later, a loud cheer sounded from inside the bus.

Part of the arrangement included the contestants staying in the bunkhouse with the crew for the first night. The crew could come and go as time allowed. They also had free run of the kitchen, dining room, and bathhouse. Carter just needed to stay out of their way.

Easy enough. He had no interest in mingling with two dozen strangers.

The contestants would be confined to the camping area after the first night.

"I'm here to start working off my debt."

He spun around to see a grumpy-looking Jay standing behind him.

"How did you get up here?" Carter hadn't heard any other vehicles making the trip up.

Jay shoved his hands into his back pockets and kicked at the ground with his worn-out tennis shoe. "What do you care?"

"How did you get here?" Carter asked again, using his "cop" voice, as his brothers called it.

Jay scowled. "Got a ride."

Carter folded his arms over his chest and stared at the boy. "From whom?"

Jay shrugged. "I don't know. Just some dude."

"You hitchhiked?" Carter narrowed his eyes at the kid. "You know that's a misdemeanor in this state?"

Jay kicked the ground again. "Bruh, relax. I didn't break no laws. He knows my old man."

Carter leaned back against the wall, frowning. "Great. Was he drunk?"

"It's okay," Jay growled, raising his hands in a

"back off" motion. "I'm real good at taking care of myself. Ain't no one gonna hurt me."

He scowled back at the kid. "You'd be surprised what kind of danger is out there for a boy your age."

Jay shrugged, his stiff stance relaxing some in obvious resignation. "Nah, I have a pretty good idea, actually."

Was that a moment of honesty by the boy or just a reflexive sarcastic jab? For some reason, it seemed more honest than sarcasm, tugging at Carter's heartstrings a little.

Carter caught Rylie watching them, a curious expression on her face as she herded her cast members from the bus and into a group she could address. As they made eye contact, she quickly looked away.

He turned back to the boy. "No more hitching rides with strangers or dudes your dad knows, okay? I'll come and get you on the weekends."

"It's no big deal. I do it all the time."

"Well, stop. As a condition of staying out of juvie, no more hitching rides. Got it?" Carter handed him a hammer. "Now help me hang this sheet of plywood over the broken window."

Jay accepted the tool with a grunt but quickly proved he knew how to handle the hammer. Every smash against the head of the nail seemed to leech some of the attitude from the boy.

Jay spoke suddenly, interrupting their silence. "I watched the big pine tree over our place the entire time it stormed. I had my backpack ready to bail. I still can't believe it didn't just fall over from the wind. Trailers aren't made so well, you know."

"That must have been very scary," Carter said. "I'm glad it didn't fall. Maybe we should take a look at it sometime, see if we can trim it up or something?"

Jay looked over at him, a hint of suspicion in his voice. "You'd do that?"

Carter nodded. "You bet, buddy."

When they finished the last few nails, Jay leaned against the boarded-up window, hands shoved into the pockets of his faded blue jeans. "That's a lot of hot women who are into camping. I never woulda thought that."

Carter set his hammer down on the table saw bench and leaned against the wood as well. "Those are contestants on a game show. A survival game show. You keep clear of them, you hear?"

"Yeah, sure." Jay shifted to rest one foot against the wall of the building, flamingo style. "A game show about survival? Who came up with such a dumb idea?"

Carter pulled his ball cap off and ran his hands through his hair. "Well, I think it was Rylie's boss. Or maybe it was *her* boss. I'm not really sure."

Jay raised an eyebrow. "Not one of those women is gonna last a week without makeup and hair-brushes. You know that, right?"

Carter nodded. "I think it's the lack of showers and using the woods as a bathroom that will do them in first. I'm not crazy about the whole thing, but the network is paying me a lot of money to let them use my property."

"Sweet." Jay shifted so his opposite foot rested against the wall and the other one stood on the ground. His expression shifted as well, from sullen to slightly amused. "Money is good. Personally, I think it's gonna be a ton of fun watching them all make fools of themselves."

"I can't want to see them try to light fires with a flint." Carter bent over and grabbed a few stray nails off the ground.

Jay nodded. "That's definitely gonna be fun."

Carter gestured toward the tools and leftover wood. "Let's get this stuff stowed in the barn, and then you can start cleaning up storm debris. The pain-in-the-a—*butt* cameraman insists on pristine conditions for filming."

He'd caught himself just in time. It may be old-school pragmaticism, but Carter wasn't going to start dropping cuss words around a fifteen-year-old kid. Somehow, someway, his mama would find out and come up the mountain to chase him down with her pump bottle of blue Dawn dish detergent.

Mama *always* found out everything, even as her five boys had grown into men, moved out, and made their way in the world. She had spies or bugs or something everywhere. Okay, so maybe she just knew every single person in Staunton and its surrounding communities, but still. Not one of the Marshall boys had *ever* gotten away with *anything*. If he'd behaved the way Jay had the past couple of years, he'd *still* be grounded.

Jay sang a song quietly to himself as he gathered up scraps of wood, a few random pieces of broken glass, and nails that had escaped the first cleanup efforts. "Where do you want me to put this stuff?"

Carter nodded toward a white bucket. "Toss it in there. I'll dump it later when I finish a couple other little projects."

Jay dropped the debris in the plastic container

and then started to walk away. "I'm gonna grab a rake and a wheelbarrow from the barn. I'll BRB."

Carter got so stuck on what BRB might mean, it didn't occur to him to question why Jay knew he had rakes and wheelbarrows in the barn.

RYLIE COULDN'T HELP but steal a glance at Carter every so often. Jay had returned. She'd seen him walking up the long drive actually looking kind of excited to get here. She had no doubt his teenaged attitude had returned the second he realized people were looking at him. Rylie already knew the boy's tough façade was just that—a wall of protection he'd created for himself.

If she weren't mistaken, Carter's own stony façade had softened just a bit when the boy showed up as well. Two tough guys who could secretly be soft and mushy on the inside.

The members of the cast chattered with loud enthusiasm all around her, returning her attention to the task at hand. Trying to get everyone matched up to their correct bags and ushered into the dorm was proving to be harder than herding cats.

"Listen up, folks!" Rylie jumped up onto the

same tree stump she'd sat on the day before. "I know everyone is super excited to be here! I am too! If you will please find your bags and make your way over to the dormitory. That's where you'll sleep tonight. It's also where we'll store your personal possessions until you either win the game or get eliminated. Once we get you settled, we'll have a meeting to explain the rules and then have some lunch."

The word *eliminated* struck up the volume of the crowd by several decibels, but at least all twelve of them started flowing toward the dorm.

Jack appeared at her side. "You sure you're ready for this?"

Rylie shrugged. "Of course. But even if I weren't, it's a little late to back out now, you know?"

"The caterer will be here in an hour to set up for lunch and dinner. Where's the host you hired?" he asked. "Wasn't he supposed to be here already?"

Rylie glanced at her smart watch. "Any minute now. I guess." She sighed with frustration. The man was late. She didn't deal well with lateness.

"I still think we should have gone with the guy who did the crazy fear show with all the bugs and stuff."

The original host Darcy chose had bailed after the whole hostage/shooting thing. Jack had been arguing for the same guy since the network had paired him with her for the show, but Rylie wanted someone new who didn't already have a television pedigree in order to keep things more authentic. Plus, he had skills of his own that would come in handy during filming.

"I like the one I've chosen." The sound of an engine revving caught her attention. "In fact, I bet that's him now. Why don't you go into the dorm and direct our contestants to settle in while I greet him."

Jack looked like he really wanted to say no but instead just walked off toward the building.

As Rylie waited, a bright orange Hummer, complete with a safari rack on top and a snorkel that rose above the roof of the vehicle, crested the hill and pulled into the clearing. Loud music emanated from the truck even with all its overly dark tinted windows closed. Two large water jugs were strapped to the back, and two even larger wooden crates had been tied to the rack up top.

Along both sides of the Hummer ran six-inch-wide stripes of camouflage paint that served about as much purpose as a bucket with a hole in it. An American flag attached to a pole on the back bumper waved in the breeze.

"Friend of yours?"

The unexpected words caused her to jump in surprise. Carter had somehow come up behind her, his approach drowned out by the thumping bass from the Hummer.

"I believe it's the host and shooting/archery instructor for the show." She motioned to the monstrosity in front of them. "I've never met him in person, but he comes highly recommended."

Carter raised an eyebrow. "By whom? Weirdos Only?"

Rylie threw her hands on her hips and leveled a glare at him. "I did *not* find my show host on a hookup app!"

He raised his eyebrow again. "So, it was an internet search, then. Makes sense."

The music turned off, ending the thumping in her chest. "You're infuriating sometimes, you know that?"

Carter chuckled quietly, surprising her.

As the Hummer's door opened, Rylie caught a solid hit of the cologne her grandfather used to wear. She resisted the urge to pinch her nose closed with her fingers even as she literally tasted the scent.

"Damn," Carter muttered.

"Mr. Flores!" Rylie extended a hand to the tall,

broad man as he unfolded himself from the truck. "Welcome! It's so wonderful to meet you."

"Howdy, *chica*!" The large man wore a cowboy hat, shiny snakeskin boots, and Wranglers. His long-sleeved camouflage shirt was partly hidden by a black tactical vest with the word INSTRUCTOR emblazoned across the chest in white. He accepted her hand and then swooped Rylie up into a big hug. "Nice to meet you, *chica*! Please, call me Carlos. Mr. Flores is my papa' and we ain't nothin' alike!"

His enthusiasm was infectious. Rylie laughed. "Nice to meet you too! So glad you could work with us. I'm excited to get started."

He tipped his cowboy hat. "I'm tickled pink to be here too."

"*Where* did you find this guy?" Carter muttered beside her. She elbowed him in the side—hard enough to make him grunt.

"Can I help you carry your things?" Rylie asked. "I'll show you to your cabin. Carter, do you have the key?"

Carter jerked a thumb in the other man's direction. "I didn't realize Clint Eastwood here was gonna need a cabin. I thought everyone would be sleeping in the dorm."

Rylie gave him her sweetest look of death. "Get

the man the key to his cabin, please. Check the contract if you have questions."

Carter raised his hands in surrender, but she could see his annoyance at another perceived inconvenience. "Yes, ma'am." He jogged off toward the office.

Rylie sighed in relief.

"How was your drive here, Mr. Flo—I mean, Carlos?" she asked, accepting a heavy duffel bag from the host.

He hefted one of the crates off the roof of the truck and set it on the ground. "Not too bad. No worse than this one time back in the war when I had to navigate fifty miles of sand in every direction with only the sun, a piece of gum, and half a bottle of water."

"That sounds challenging." Rylie saw Jay and waved him over, doing her absolute best to hide the burst of laughter trying to break free. The man looked totally serious.

Jay jogged right over to them, a huge smile of admiration on his face as he took in the orange monstrosity on wheels. When he reached them, Jay properly adjusted his smile to a scowl. "Sweet ride."

"Why, thank you, young man." Carlos hoisted

the other crate off the luggage rack. "You think you can carry the one on the ground?"

"Yeah." Jay grabbed the crate with both hands and hardly any effort. The boy was definitely stronger than he looked.

"Impressive, young man." To Rylie he said, "Show me the way to my new digs."

As she led the way toward the camp office, wondering where Carter was with the key, he stepped out of the building.

"Which one you want him in?" Jay asked.

"Four." He motioned to the cabin behind Jack's. "I haven't been in there in a while, though. I didn't realize I needed to have three ready."

Carlos shrugged. "Son, I've slept in foxholes in the jungle covered with banana leaves and mosquitos. Monkeys threw their dung at me for fun. A little dust ain't gonna bother me none."

"Wow! You have had such an exciting life!" Jay said, looking at him in awe.

Carlos waved him off. "It wasn't all that."

"Well, I'm just glad you were able to fit our show into your schedule. I know how busy you must be." Rylie was also confused by Carlos's anecdotes, but he wasn't there to give his life story. She needed him to teach the dormitory full of rookie survivalists how to bow hunt and trap and make their own shelter. That was it.

"I've never been up here in the Blue Ridge Mountains. I'm lookin' forward to teaching the city folk how to live the cowboy life."

They stopped in front of the cabin. Carter, who had said nothing the past few minutes, stuck the key in the lock and pushed the door open. Rylie heard him mumble, "Now he's a cowboy. Sounds more like multiple personality disorder to me."

Rylie shot him yet another glare and went into the cabin. "Home sweet home. For the next few weeks anyway."

Carlos plowed his way into the cabin, boots stomping the whole way. Once inside, he dropped the crate he carried. Jay set the other one on top of it, and Rylie set the duffel bag on the bed. The mattress was bare.

"Jay, run to the barn and get the cowboy here a sleeping bag." Carter must have read her mind.

"On it." Jay sauntered off.

"He's loving this," Rylie said as they all watched him go.

"How you figure? He's all attitude at every turn." Carter looked over at her, an eyebrow raised.

Rylie shrugged. "it's obvious. Weren't you a detective once or something?"

"That your boy? Y'all made a handsome kid," Carlos said, pulling off his hat and hanging it on a hook by the door.

"Jay isn't ours." Carter looked like he might blow a series of gaskets at the thought of having a kid with her.

Rylie shook her head vehemently. "We aren't a couple. We pretty much just met. I mean, we sort of met before, but.... We don't have anything in common anyway. He's not even my type." She knew she was rambling but couldn't stop. Her new show host just looked at her in amusement.

Carter, however, was anything but amused. "I'm sure the man has better things to do than to listen to you carry on about how much you don't like me." He might have even sounded like his ego was a little bit bruised.

"I never said—"

Jay came flying into the little cabin, face flushed and totally out of breath. He carried a sleeping bag under each arm. "I didn't know which one you would prefer—a regular or a cold weather one." He held them out to Carlos. "The mountains get pretty cold at night this time of year."

Carlos gestured to the bed. "Just drop them both on the bunk over there, and I'll figure it out later. I've slept outside during a raging blizzard with nothing but a poncho and an old carboard box. This here is like the Four Seasons for me."

A tiny hint of hero worship sparked in Jay's eyes. "You've sure done some crazy sh—"

Carlos laughed, drowning out the rest of Jay's sentence.

Beside her, Carter scoffed. "Desert, jungle, and now the tundra? Dude's got some tall tales. You should never trust the reviews online. Probably had his mama and grandma write them."

Only Rylie heard him. Carlos continued on with the newest story he'd spun for Jay.

Her phone chimed. She pulled it from her pocket and scowled at Jack's name on the screen.

> Jack: I need you over here right now.

> Rylie: Whatever it is, just handle it.

> Jack: There's about to be a brawl over which woman gets to sleep next to the hot guy. I'm not equipped to handle that. AT ALL.

> Rylie: Fine! I'll be right there.

She shoved the phone back into her jeans pocket. "If you could excuse me, Carlos, I'm needed in the dormitory to break up a girl fight."

Jay's face completely lit up. "Can I help?" he asked enthusiastically.

Carter clapped him on the shoulder. "Calm down there, buddy. Let Ms. Christianson handle this. It's her show."

Jay shoved his hands into his pockets and scowled. "Dude, it's a *girl fight*. Those don't just happen every day."

"I promise you can meet the cast later," Rylie assured him as she headed toward the dorm.

CHAPTER THIRTEEN

"She's a feisty one." Carlos pulled the lid off one of the wooden crates. "She didn't give me the chance to even say no to this gig. Not that I would have. Have you seen the amazing view?" He pointed toward the fall colors outside his window.

Carter rolled his eyes. "Yeah, I've seen it once or twice. The kid and I got some work to do. We had a fire and a storm yesterday."

He motioned for Jay to follow him out of the cabin.

"Busy day for y'all. Did the storm start the fire? That musta been some light show!" Carlos called after them.

"I really wish I'd kept my big mouth shut," Carter said as they walked away.

"About what?" Jay asked.

"So many things, kid. So. Many. Things." He headed toward the storage barn to grab some rakes, shovels, and a couple wheelbarrows. "Let's get to work on the fire mess. Let the storm debris sit."

As they neared the barn, a shrill scream pierced the quiet mountain air.

"Did you hear that?" Jay asked, his voice filled with fear. "That's all wrong for a girl fight."

A second scream sounded. Pretty sure it was Rylie this time, Carter took off at a run toward the dormitory. As he neared the building, a horde of people came flooding out the double doors. Some were yelling, others crying. They all looked completely terrified.

"What happened?" he asked everyone he passed, but no one could tell him.

Jay followed close behind. As Carter reached the doors, he stopped and turned to the boy. "Stay out here."

Jay looked like he wanted to argue, but he kept his mouth shut and just nodded. Carter plowed through the double doors and into the dormitory. A scent he'd experienced too many times before hit him.

The building held the scent of fresh death.

Carter sucked in a breath. This was not going to be good.

"Rylie!" He spotted her in a corner of the long room, looking down at one of the cots. Jack stood beside her, his skin completely void of any color.

Carter ran over to where they stood and immediately wished he hadn't. On top of the narrow bed lay a man. He was covered by a wool blanket up to his neck. Both of his arms hung off the sides of the cot, his hands grazing the floor. There was a small pool of scarlet beneath his head under the bed that had begun to trail toward the wall. The blood hadn't really begun to congeal yet, so he hadn't been dead very long.

He turned to Jack and Rylie. "Do either of you know him?"

Rylie, tears streaming down her face, nodded. "Yes. We both do. He's one of the writers for the show. We are—were—friends."

She covered her face with her hands as a sob racked her entire body.

"Why don't you get her out of here, Jack?" Carter motioned toward the door. "I've got to call this in."

Carter did not relish the thought of having to call the dispatcher again. This would be the second time in three days—that didn't look so good for him.

None of it looked good.

Rylie's car and the dead owl, the cabin fire, someone attacking Rylie, and now a possible murder? What in the name of all things holy was happening on his mountain?

He pulled his phone from his pocket and dialed 911.

"911. What's your emergency?" Of course, it had to be the same operator who'd answered when he called the first time.

He took a deep breath to steady his voice. "Lani, it's Carter Marshall."

"Marshall! This is becoming a thing. What's going on?" She sounded a little concerned.

Yeah, well, he was too.

"There's been an accident, I guess. Appears to be a head injury. One of the crew members for the show filming here this month."

He heard the clicking of her keyboard as she typed in the call. "I'm sending police and EMS."

Carter sighed. "You better just send the medical examiner and crime scene instead. EMS can't do anything. He's cold."

Silence filled the space between them for a full ten seconds. "How awful. I'm so sorry."

What she didn't say was *"What the heck is happening up there?"*

A question he heard very clearly in her voice and one he'd very much like to have the answer to as well.

"How long till they can get here, Lani?" he finally asked. "I have a lot of very upset people here."

"There's nothing active on the books right now, so expect them within the hour. I'm sending an ambulance and patrol units ahead, just to verify and pronounce." He heard more clicking of the keyboard. "For now, you know the drill. Protect the scene. Keep people away."

"Already on it."

After ending the call, Carter stowed his phone in the back pocket of his jeans. The entire thing was absolutely unreal. What kind of chaos had descended on his property?

The most immediate issue was where to put the cast and crew of Rylie's show for the night. His dormitory would be off-limits for the investigation. There were plenty of sleeping bags. He and Jay could clear the dining hall and put out sleeping bags for the cast, and the rest of the crew could share the last four empty cabins.

With an outline of a plan in mind, Carter walked toward the double doors, stopping to make sure the other two entrances were still secure. As he pushed through the exit to the crowd waiting outside, he caught sight of a very shaken Rylie being comforted by a very smug Jack.

The cast and crew gathered in groups, many animatedly discussing the dead man in the building. Jay was off to the side, seemingly overwhelmed. Carter waved him over. Jay immediately looked relieved as he jogged to where Carter stood.

"Rylie and Jack say a guy was murdered in there." Jay's relief had transitioned to worry.

Carter shook his head. "We don't know that. It looks like he could have just hit his head and didn't feel so great, so he lay down. One of the crew members. I called it in. EMS and Crime Scene will be here soon. In the meantime, I need your help with something, Jay."

"Anything." Jay rocked back on his heels, his hands shoved into his pockets. "I need something to do."

Carter studied the boy, concerned. "On second thought, maybe I should send you home. You could be in danger up here."

Jay shook his head. "It's fine. Really. I can take care of myself."

Off in the distance, sirens from an ambulance sounded. The whole team would be there soon. They needed to get the crowd relocated and quick.

"Can you go to the barn and bring back all the sleeping bags? Put them in a wheelbarrow and bring them straight to the dining hall. These people are gonna need a place to crash tonight. As soon as I can, though, I'm taking you home."

"I got you!" Jay took off running toward the barn, ignoring the last bit.

A second set of sirens, from a police cruiser, clashed with the ones from the ambulance. The entire place was about to be a crazy hot mess if he didn't get these people into the dining hall.

"Jack!" He hated to even say the other man's name, but times were desperate.

Jack glanced over at him, an arm still wrapped around Rylie's shoulders.

Carter's fists clenched, desperate to get a piece of the other man's jaw, but he maintained his self-control.

"Jack! Bring Rylie and come here!"

Thin lipped, Jack nodded once, then whispered something to Rylie. Together they walked over to where Carter waited. Well, Rylie walked. Jack sauntered like he'd won some big prize in a competition only he had taken part in.

All around them, fear settled in thick.

"Did anyone see the body?" one cast member asked, sounding more excited than maybe he should have.

"I heard he had his throat slit wide open!" another replied.

A young woman with too much makeup on for a survival camp wrapped her arms around herself and shivered. "After what happened the first time they tried to make this show, I never should have agreed to come back. I need to get off this mountain."

The woman standing next to her laughed. "Just pretend you're on one of those true crime shows you love to watch."

"What in the name of flying monkeys is going on here?" Carlos, the show host, bellowed across the crowd. He'd changed his cowboy hat for a bright safety-orange knit cap that served as a beacon atop the tall man.

People began to turn toward him, eyeing the stranger—perhaps hoping he held the answers to all their questions.

"Great. Just what we need," Carter mumbled as

Rylie and Jack approached. "Someone needs to rein him in. We don't need his wild storytelling stirring the pot right now." He looked pointedly at Jack. "How about you go deal with him. Rylie and I will get everyone into the dining hall."

The sirens were getting louder. They'd be at the campground in a matter of minutes. The level of chatter increased in volume as people started looking around for the source of the noise.

"Go. Now." Carter barely resisted the urge to shove Jack toward the man who had already gathered a small crowd around him.

"How about we drop their things in the building, and I'll take the cast to the firepit area for some preshow discussion?" Rylie asked.

"I've got a better idea," Jack countered. "Let's use the giant over there to lead the crowd away like he's the Pied Piper."

Carter hated to admit it, but the jerk had a solid suggestion. "Fine. Let them take their bags with them. Jay and I will get the dining hall rearranged. We'll pull some tables outside for meals."

"Okay." Rylie nodded. "Come on, Jack. Let's get them out of here."

She jogged off toward their show host. Jack followed. Carter watched as Rylie said something to

Carlos, who turned and sauntered off in the direction of the newly constructed firepit along with her and Jack, the rest of the group following like a herd of cats chasing a laser dot.

No sooner had they moved on than the ambulance and police car crested the hill of the drive, moving at very unsafe speeds.

He growled when he realized the cruiser was the unmarked vehicle of Detective Peters, back on his mountain again.

Ignoring him, Carter jogged over to the ambulance once it had parked in the center of the compound. The driver cut the engine and jumped from the cab.

"Hey! Slow down! The body is already getting cold. He's been dead a couple hours at least. He's not going anywhere."

His partner, a much younger man, came around the back of the truck, hauling a large orange jump bag. "What're you standing around for, Ellis? Your ticker finally decided to give up the ghost?"

"Aren't you the *not* funny one, Matty. Act like a professional, kid, or I'll tell your mama." Shoving his cap back onto his head, he motioned toward Carter. "Hoss here says we're looking at a cold one. No need to rush now. He's not gettin' any deader."

"You damn near killed us both for nothing?" The younger medic, Matty, looked madder than a wet hornet at his partner.

Peters ambled over to where they stood, a satisfied grin on his face. "So, Marshall, this show thing turned out to be a real great idea, didn't it? What's the city council going to think about all this criminal activity happening on the property of a former cop? Finally, a Marshall brother who isn't the department's golden boy."

"Seriously, Peters?"

The detective shrugged. "Truth hurt, pretty boy?"

"How about you all follow me, and I'll take you to the victim." Carter strode toward the dorm, hoping the distraction was enough to prevent an all-out fight.

The two medics bickered all the way into the building. Carter led them to the cot in the far corner where the body lay.

Carter had seen his fair share of bodies. Usually, he could keep a little separation between himself and the victim. This one happening on his watch at his campground, though—it hit different.

He pointed at the man on the cot. "I think he whacked his head pretty hard on something."

"Or someone whacked it for him," Matty said as he imitated swinging a baseball bat.

"Do y'all think maybe we could show a little respect for the deceased?"

Carter nodded, as Peters had finally said something useful. "I agree with the detective. This man probably has a family, you know?" He stepped around the cot to the opposite side. "I think maybe he was ambushed."

The door opened, then closed as a familiar voice spoke. "How 'bout we let the scientist figure it out. Nothing tells the truth like scientific evidence."

"Vonda." Carter turned and nodded at the crime scene tech. "Nice to see you again. Just wish it weren't so soon."

Her smile was understanding, but she remained all business. "I'm not sure what's going on up here, but I think maybe you've got an enemy."

Carter frowned. "I have a lot of enemies, I'm sure. But I don't think I've ever driven anyone to murder."

"You said it yourself—can't say for sure this *was* murder. Not until the ME gets him on the table." Vonda set her kit down and opened it up. "It's not looking good for you, though. Someone has a grudge, and they're making a huge statement about it. I'd watch your back, Marshall." She pulled on her customary Tyvek suit, gloves, and face mask.

"Sorry, Marshall, but you're gonna have to step out. You can't investigate this one." Peters pulled a pack of gum from his shirt pocket, unwrapped a piece, and popped it into his mouth. "Just like everyone else up here, you're a possible suspect."

"Are you freaking kidding me?" Carter resisted the urge to growl at the other man. "The guy hit his head! On my property. I have to make sure this gets figured out."

"You know how it goes." Peters snapped the piece of gum he'd been chewing on. "Your property, no one saw what happened—kinda puts you at the top of the list, don't it?" He stepped in close enough that Carter could feel the heat of the other man's breath.

"You know that's ridiculous." Carter stepped back, putting space between them again.

"Peters." Vonda narrowed her eyes at the detective. "You can't really think Marshall would have anything to do with this?"

"Maybe. Maybe not." Peters shrugged and nodded toward the door. "Now go before you contaminate the scene even more."

"Peters—"

"Seems to me like you two got some kinda personal thing going on here." Ellis pulled his cap off and rubbed his head again. "I think y'all should work on that later. We have a body that really needs to be secured and transported."

The medic was right, and Carter could see that Peters knew it too. He held his hands up in mock surrender. "I'll leave you all to it."

As he walked away, Carter heard Ellis say, "Matty and I agree, the man is dead. I'll call it in. Is the medical examiner on the way?"

The door slammed behind him as he exited the building, cutting off any response by Peters. He made absolutely no effort to stop it either. The crash echoed the level of his aggravation at the detective.

CHAPTER FOURTEEN

"ALL RIGHT NOW! EVERYONE, PLEASE HAVE A seat!" Rylie cupped her hands together like a little megaphone. "Pull up a log and sit down!"

A hand on her shoulder caught her off guard. Spinning around, already in fight-or-flight mode, she calmed down considerably when she saw it was the show host, Carlos.

"Want me to give it a try? Nothing says 'pay attention' like a six-foot-two Puerto Rican in a bright orange hat, snakeskin boots, and a flak vest." He gave her a contagious smile that relaxed her even more.

She had definitely made the right choice for show host. His calming demeanor would be an asset throughout the filming process.

"This is not the way to start filming a new show," Jack said, his irritation more than obvious.

She leveled an angry glare at her assistant. "Not helping, Jack. You should be filming some of this."

"Whatever." He busied himself messing with his camera gear.

Rylie jumped up onto one of the logs and gave a nod to Mr. Flores, who stepped up onto the log beside her. As predicted, even before he spoke, the roar of the crowd simmered to a low hum.

"If y'all could just settle on down for a minute and let our *chica* talk, I'd sure appreciate it. I know this is super upsetting, but someone is dead, and we need to respect that right now. All this chittin' and chattin' and fearmongerin' ain't gonna help."

A complete hush fell over the crowd as they scrambled for seats. Jack was right—Carlos did have an interesting hold over the crowd.

Once everyone had settled down, Rylie spoke. "Thank you all for accommodating this unexpected turn of events. I'm so sorry to anyone who had to see... what happened. The police and EMS are here taking care of things."

"Who got killed?" a woman asked. "Maybe we should leave. I mean, after what happened the last time we tried to do this...."

Her voice trailed off into a murmur that reverberated through the crowd.

"We don't know for sure anyone was murdered." Rylie said, trying to sound confident. "He may have just hit his head. Accidents happen all the time at campgrounds. If the police tell us to leave, we will, but for now, we'll stick to the production schedule."

"So, you're trying to tell us that the man hit his head, then died tucked in on a cot?" a man called out as he looked around the group seated on logs. "Was he one of the contestants?"

"Nope," Jack said, shrugging. "One of our crew. And I have no idea what happened to him. The police will investigate."

The nonchalance and lack of emotion in Jack's voice sent a chill through her. How could he be so calm and disinterested?

Carlos seemed surprised by it, too, as he raised an eyebrow at the cameraman in question. "You good, *ese*?"

Jack ignored him, which didn't surprise Rylie at all.

Jay passed through her line of sight, pushing a large wheelbarrow full of sleeping bags. He headed in the direction of the dining hall. Good. They would be able to get the cast settled soon.

"Mr. Marshall, the owner of the property and our sponsor, is busy clearing out the dining hall building for you all to store your things and spend the night in. As you know, we don't hit the primitive sites until tomorrow. Today we have some preproduction stuff to take care of, and the caterer will be here to serve lunch and dinner. Nothing changes."

"So, life goes on as if nothing happened?" This question came from a crew member. "Mikey's life doesn't matter? All we care about is staying on production schedule?"

"That's not true at all," Rylie replied. "It's a terrible tragedy, but until we know more or the police tell us otherwise, things continue on the way they were planned."

"I want to go home," someone called out.

"This show is cursed!" another person said. "I knew I should have pulled out!"

"I don't want to be out here in the middle of nowhere. Can we cancel?"

Rylie pursed her lips as she listened to all the comments. Obviously, they were afraid. Especially the ones who'd been on scene last time. But if she could push past this accident, she knew they would all be fine. Emotions were running high, and rightfully so, but Rylie felt confident things would calm down by the next morning. If the show missed filming again, there would no more show. Darcy's dream would be gone. All of it just *gone*.

"Mikey's death matters," Rylie continued, raising her voice over the crowd. "It was a terrible accident, and he will be missed greatly. I know this feels like a bad omen after what happened at the original site, but this is different. I assure you, we are all perfectly safe. Our host is a retired cop—he knows what to do in an emergency situation."

The crowd murmured an array of agreement and understanding in response to what she said.

"I feel like Mikey would want us to go ahead with the show," the same crew member who had shouted out earlier said. "We should do this in his memory. And Darcy's."

The rest of the crew nodded and voiced agreement, as did the cast members.

"So, we're good, then." Relief washed through her. "This is our host, Carlos. He has a ton of experience and is excited to get to know you all."

Carlos pulled his hat off and waved it in the air. "I'm mighty glad to be here. It's a damn shame what happened to that young fella." He slung an arm around her shoulders. "When Miss Rylie here contacted me about this show, I just knew I had to do it. We're gonna have a great time. I can feel it in my gut. So, who's ready to do this thing?"

The crowd sent up a round of cheers and clapping.

Jack raised his camera and turned on the filming light. "Everyone smile and wave for the camera!"

He walked around with the camera, interviewing contestants while Rylie gathered the other half dozen crew members. "Mr. Marshall is going to put all of you in cabins. You'll be bunking two to a cabin. It'll be tight, but hopefully only for a day or two. Word of warning—they're *very* rustic."

"But what about Mikey's... body?" the same crew member who had spoken of him previously approached her and asked.

"The police are taking care of things. I'll notify the network, and they'll reach out to his family. I'll ask for some extra security too."

"It's awful," someone else said. "He was the nicest guy alive. He's definitely gonna be missed."

The man was right about Mikey. They'd gone out a few times, and everything about him was just nice and kind.

One of the cast members, a tall, thin red-haired female, walked up to them and thumbed in the direction of the remains of the cabin behind them. "What happened there?"

If Rylie remembered correctly, she actually worked as a wildfire firefighter on the West Coast. Made sense that she'd ask about the rubble.

"An accident. We had some rough storms roll through." So what if maybe the fire and the storms were completely unrelated. It wouldn't serve any purpose to share that with all the fearful people looking to her for answers. "Mountain storms are nasty. I'm sure we'll have one or two during filming. Something to think about as your teams work on shelters."

"Hmmm... a storm. If you say so." The woman didn't seem convinced, but there wasn't time to dissect the incident. She had to go through the rules and a million other details before the caterers arrived and were ready to serve up lunch.

THE FLAMES DANCED SLOWLY against the backdrop of the dark night. The cast had been sent to their quarters about twenty minutes earlier after their very first campfire meeting, in which Rylie showed them what the process would be like during filming and then turned it over to their show host.

Carlos had enamored the cast with his quick wit and sunny personality. His eccentric appearance seemed to endear him to them. He definitely had some personality quirks too. The odd man who would become the face of her show was just perfect for the job.

Jack and the rest of the crew had gone into town to burn off some of the excess energy from the traumatic events of the day.

Now, she sat alone in the cold night air, waiting for the fire to die out while contemplating sleep herself.

"Hey." Carter appeared out of the darkness, the fire illuminating his silhouette. He carried a brown paper sack in one hand as he walked over to where she sat. "Jay's old man was out cold when I dropped him off."

"Is that good or bad?"

Carter settled on the log beside her, his long, muscular legs stretched out until his boots were nearly at the stone fire ring. "After the day I've had, it's very good. If he'd started anything, I might have spent the night under arrest in my former precinct."

He laughed without humor. "It's been one hell of a day."

Rylie leaned toward him, lightly bumping his shoulder with her own. "I know this whole show thing isn't easy for you."

"Understatement of the year." There was no mistaking the heavy sarcasm clinging to those words. It made Rylie feel really bad. Carter didn't deserve any of the things happening at the campground. If she discovered she was in any way responsible, it would wreck her.

"I don't know what's happening here—or why— but I can have the network send out some security to help out if you want me to?"

Carter shook his head as he reached into the paper bag and pulled out two bottles of beer. He handed one to Rylie. Not usually her drink of choice, her mouth suddenly watered at the thought of the ice-cold liquid nonetheless. "Not yet. I'd rather not bring outsiders in when it's my own department working on this. If it was an accident, there's no need to worry everyone."

"Okay," Rylie said, letting the topic drop for the moment.

He popped the cap off his bottle with an opener on his key ring and took a long sip of his drink before handing her the bottle opener. "The whole show thing is *not* easy. I'm an introvert who craves peace and solitude, not chaos. But I can deal with chaos. It's the fire, and you getting attacked, and now a dead man on my property that I'm struggling with. I may not be a cop officially anymore, but I can't shake the training, you know? These things aren't supposed to happen to someone like me."

Rylie opened her own bottle and set the keys on the log between them. "None of this is happening to you. It's happening on your property."

Carter frowned. For a moment she worried she'd crossed a line. She could make out the sharp planes of his features in the firelight as his expression morphed to sadness.

She nudged his arm with her elbow. "I'm sorry. Mikey's death is really weighing on me. I worry it wasn't an accident."

"I know. I only said it was to keep your cast members calm. But it doesn't sit well with me at all." He sighed, his shoulders drooping heavily. "I hope he didn't have a wife or kids."

She shook her head. "No. He wasn't married. But his parents are elderly and depend on him a lot. This is gonna kill them."

"You were friends." It was a statement, not a question.

"Yeah, I guess we were."

A tear escaped the corner of her right eye. Rylie swiped at it but not fast enough. Carter saw the quick movement and gave her a questioning look. "More than friends?"

"We dated once or twice, but we just never clicked in that way, you know?" Rylie took a long drink from the bottle she held. "He was a really great guy. Just not the right guy for me, I guess. The really great ones never are."

Carter took a long swallow of his beer, finishing it. Tossing the empty bottle beside the bag, he pulled out another. When he reached for the bottle opener, his large hand landed on hers. The heat emanating from him warmed her very soul as he let his fingers rest lightly on hers. The tension built between them until it damn near crackled alongside the fire.

Since he didn't move, she didn't either. Rylie leaned into him, resting against his shoulder. Carter wrapped her hand in his.

"Your fingers are freezing," he said quietly, his breath warm on her ear.

"I get cold easily." She pointed up at the patch of dark sky above the clearing. "The stars were so

perfect. I couldn't bring myself to go inside. Especially after a day like this."

"The night sky up here is like a work of art. I've
never seen anything like it, anywhere I've been."

"I know exactly what you mean. We have too
many city lights in Los Angeles to see any stars at
all." A light breeze kicked up, causing a shiver to pass
through her.

Carter let go of her hand. Rylie felt the loss of his
touch like a kick to the gut. He picked up the keys
from the log and shifted closer, though, and then he
wrapped an arm around her. His warmth engulfed
her immediately. Snuggling in close, Rylie rested her
head on his shoulder and sighed. It had been so long
since she'd had the comfort of another person's touch.

"Better?" he asked, sounding incredibly tenta-
tive. Like maybe he shouldn't have been so forward
and wanted to know it was okay.

She smiled up at him. "Much. It must be nice to
run so hot. I'm like a walking iceberg most of the
time."

"My mama always said Marshall men were like
furnaces. She and Dad couldn't do the whole cuddle-
sleep thing at night because it was just too hot."

Rylie giggled. "That's good information to have if

we ever get trapped in an underground cave or walk-in freezer."

Carter chuckled as well. "I guess maybe it was a little too much information." He sounded more than a touch embarrassed.

He tried to pull away a little, but Rylie slid in closer, not about to let one degree of his body heat escape her. Reaching out, she linked their fingers. She enjoyed the roughness of his hand against her icy skin.

"Nope. Not at all. It's actually the most normal thing anyone has said to me in weeks. I guess it just adds to the weirdness of this whole experience, doesn't it?"

One of the logs shifted in the fire, dropping into the center and kicking up a shower of sparks. The tiny orange lights floated down all around the firepit, a stark contrast to the darkness they invaded. She watched as they settled, their tiny lights going out on contact with the damp ground.

"I actually understand better than you think." Carter exhaled softly.

There was such sadness in his voice, Rylie wrapped an arm around his waist and hugged him. Deciding this was as good a time as any to address the elephant between them, she said, "You know Darcy dying wasn't your fault, right?"

He stiffened. "You remember things differently than I do, I guess."

She turned to look at him. "I remember a cop—a *really* good cop—doing everything he could to save the hostages. You saved a lot of lives that night."

He took her hand and tucked it into the pocket of his flannel coat. "It's the one I lost who haunts me." Carter stared at the fire, his expression stoic.

Rylie tried to think of something to say to make him feel better, but she came up empty. The only one who could make him feel better was Carter himself.

"Sometimes things just happen no matter how hard we try to stop them. You were injured. What more could you have done?"

He exhaled deeply. "Yeah, well, I don't believe in fate or destiny or whatever you want to call it."

There was obviously no convincing him that some things just couldn't be stopped once the universe put them in motion. "Darcy was a real cool woman. You'd have liked her. She could hold her own in almost any situation, no matter what."

Carter shrugged. "What kind of a cop lets someone like Darcy get murdered?"

Rylie jumped to her feet and stood in front of him so he was forced to look at her. "Her death is on her killer, not you! I really try not to, but I also blame myself, you know. Sometimes I wonder—maybe if I'd been there, I could have saved her somehow."

He scoffed, tossing a stick into the flames. "That's just crazy. How could you have protected her from an armed man hell-bent on killing her?"

"Did you know he had a sealed record?" Rylie asked, lowering her voice.

"Who?" Carter looked confused.

"Mason. The guy who shot Darcy. He wasn't right in the head." Rylie pulled the hood of her jacket up against a bitter wind gust. She took a step back, and her foot landed on a rock. As her ankle rolled, Rylie stumbled toward the fire. As she plunged forward, arms flailing, fear rendered her mute. She tried to cry out but couldn't make a sound. It all happened so fast.

Strong hands gripped her waist hard, yanking her back from the fire. Rylie crashed against Carter's large frame.

When her knees buckled, Rylie fell toward the ground again. Carter spun her around, wrapping her in a tight bear hug. The rush of adrenaline set her fight-or-flight response into overdrive, causing her entire body to quake as her pulse rushed in her ears.

"It's okay. You're okay." Carter smoothed her hair with one hand as he held her close. "Let the adrenaline run its course."

Rylie reached up and wrapped her arms around his neck, letting Carter's strength keep her upright. She buried her face in the soft fabric of his flannel jacket. "I'm so sorry. I don't even know how that happened."

Carter rested his chin on her hair. She thought he maybe even pressed a light kiss to the top of her head. "There's nothing to apologize for. You tripped. Could have happened to anyone. I'm just glad I caught you before you got hurt."

Rylie smiled against his chest, enjoying the sensation of his arms around her. It made her feel safe and a little something else she wasn't ready to evaluate yet. "You saved my life. Actually, that's at least twice now that you've saved me." She waved her fingers in the air that had hit the griddle a few days before. "See? You are a hero."

He smoothed her hair down and pulled the hood of her jacket back up. "I'm not a hero. Just a regular guy who happened to be at the right place at the right time to catch a beautiful woman. Twice."

His voice had gone incredibly gruff. So much so, Rylie felt its roughness right to her core. Snaking her arms around his waist, she rested her cheek against his chest once more. "You were a good cop, and you're a great man with a serious confidence issue. I'm making it my mission to change that."

They held each for a long time. The fire ceased to give off much heat as it burned down to coals. It didn't matter to her. Rylie was warmed all the way through.

"You've stopped shaking." Carter released his hold on her.

She immediately felt the chill of his absence. Wrapping her arms around herself to try and hold on to the warmth, she winked at him. "Marshall men run hot. I told you that would be important knowledge to have."

Carter cleared his throat. "You better get some rest. Tomorrow's going to be a big day for you."

Rylie nodded. "You know, I wasn't even on-site when Darcy's fiancé lost his mind, threatening to kill all the invaders on his land. I had a flat tire coming into town. Thankfully, a nice older man who reminded me of my own father gave up a good thirty minutes of his time to change it for me on the side of the Blue Ridge Parkway."

Which meant she'd shown up once the SWAT team was already in place and Carter had begun negotiations with Mason.

He reached up and toyed with a piece of her hair. "It's not your fault either. I hope you realize that."

She smiled up at him, longing to bury herself in his warmth again. "I guess we both need to work on the self-blame."

The sound of a vehicle engine working far too hard broke the peace of the night. Headlights soon cast a glow over the forest, chasing away the darkness and the tension that had built between them.

"I'm guessing that's your boyfriend and his crew," Carter said, stepping away from her.

Why did he keep insisting Jack was her boyfriend? Carter Marshall could be absolutely infuriating.

"Jack is *not* my boyfriend. He is a colleague. One I don't even really like all that much. Just so you know." Rylie started walking toward the cabins. "Do yourself a favor, Carter. Stop blaming yourself for things you can't control. Carrying the weight of the world is not a one-man job."

CHAPTER FIFTEEN

CARTER FINISHED OFF THE REST OF THE BEERS AS he watched the coals die away until all that remained was ash. He'd felt Rylie's absence the moment she jumped up from the log. The peace he'd experienced with her tucked in against his side had chased away the demons for a little bit. Telling the story about his parents had surprised him. Rylie seemed to like it, though. Being with her felt comfortable. Until her boss's death came up and changed everything. Her parting words hit him harder than he'd like to admit —the peace and comfort instantly replaced with guilt and anger at himself.

What did she know about him or his life anyway? She was a city girl playing mountain survivor for a television show. Carter lived on the mountain, had made it his livelihood. Rylie Christianson didn't know a damn thing about him.

She had no idea that he rarely slept anymore, or how images of that day haunted him every time he closed his eyes. His own near-death experience—she'd never understand that either.

He'd never be able to get that day out of his head. Quitting his job hadn't helped. Isolating himself from the world and his family hadn't helped. Her presence, a constant reminder of his massive failure in getting shot and losing the victim, definitely wasn't helping.

The fact that he was really starting to enjoy her presence also did absolutely nothing for his damaged being.

Carter dumped the rest of the last beer on the hot ash, watching the steam disappear into the night and leaving him as dark on the outside as he felt on the inside.

He spent the rest of the night and the next several days keeping his distance from the reality show—and Rylie. They were too comfortable together. She felt familiar and almost made him believe it was okay to be happy. Something he'd lost the right to feel on that fateful day.

His encounter with Rylie had stirred up so many

feelings and emotions about so many things that the only way he knew how to deal was by not doing so. By Friday night, sleep had been so elusive, he'd almost given up on it completely.

On Saturday morning, the fragrance of frying bacon woke him from a fitful sleep. He'd finally drifted off at around three thirty. Then the nightmares came. When he opened one eye to check, the clock on his phone read 6:20 a.m. Carter groaned, his breath making a little cloud in his cold cabin. What little rest he'd gotten had been filled with memories of that day. Only instead of Darcy lying dead in that house, it had been Rylie.

The image of her blood-covered body sent a chill through him even the temperature in the cabin couldn't outdo.

They hadn't spoken much since the night by the fire. The first week of filming was nearly over, and so far—knock on wood—nothing else had happened.

Of course, they still had no idea what happened to the crew member. Carter's gut told him it was murder, but forensics turned up nothing to support anything but an accident. Neither had the police interviews. Vonda's theory had involved a walk in the woods where he fell and hit his head. She figured he'd tucked himself into bed, hoping to sleep off the headache, and never woke up.

Carter didn't buy into it, though. Yeah, Vonda was the best at what she did, but given the previous incidents, he couldn't help but think something else had happened. With no forensics or investigative evidence to support *his* theory, though, he stayed quiet. For now.

Some of the show people had started whispering about suicide and life insurance. Rylie sometimes seemed content to let them believe what they wanted to keep the peace among the cast and get her show filmed. He wanted to discuss it with her but had held back. The urge to interview cast members and follow up any leads was strong, but he held back on that as well. The department had made it crystal clear that he needed to stay out of it. He was no longer a cop, and it would do him good to remember that.

His reputation hadn't been the same since the incident either. That was how he'd started to refer to it in his head. The plan had been to box up and stash away the entire event to help him get past it.

Although, based on the dream he'd just had, it wasn't working out so well at the moment.

As he sat up, the icy air in the cabin hit his bare chest, raising some serious gooseflesh along his arms.

Carter kicked off the wool blanket and stood up. After pulling on some jeans, a waffle-knit crew-neck shirt, and a pair of heavy socks as quickly as he could manage, he shoved his feet into his boots and pulled on a fleece-lined jean jacket. As he left the cabin, Carter shoved a knit hat on his head and stuffed his hands into his pockets.

The smell of bacon and eggs wrapped him in a delicious-smelling hug. A group of crew members gathered near a food truck that hadn't been on the property the night before.

Laughter permeated the light fog embracing the campground. Carter caught sight of Rylie standing with Jack. A couple uniformed officers milled about with the crew. Peters had texted that he was going to have officers on-site overnight and throughout the day, just in case.

Grumbling, Carter walked to the office and let himself in. The lights were on, and he could hear Josh talking to himself in the office. The only one in his family he still saw or talked to regularly was Josh.

"Hey, little brother." Carter leaned against the doorframe.

Josh had an overflowing plate of food on his desk. "Have you tried this stuff? It's freaking delicious. Those TV people sure know how to eat." He shoved a piece of toast loaded with scrambled eggs into his mouth.

Carter scowled. Everything about the television show rubbed him the wrong way. "It's just food, Josh. You eat every day. I've seen you make that exact meal dozens of times. *I've* made you that same meal more than once."

Josh shrugged and picked up a piece of bacon. "I guess it just tastes better when it comes out of a truck."

He moaned as he ate the bacon. Carter shook his head and walked back out of the cabin. Yellow crime scene tape had been wrapped around the dormitory all week. Peters had told him he could remove it, but Carter had left it as a way to keep people out of the building. The crime felt unresolved to him, so he didn't want to mess with the scene just yet.

The show was one-third of the way through the contract. He could stay out of the way for two more weeks. Then Rylie Christianson would be gone, and he would have a big fat check from the network.

"Mr. Marshall."

Carter turned to see Jay standing behind him with a heaping plate of food, a piece of bacon in one hand.

"What do you need me to do today?"

Jay had come to the mountain a dour, miserable force with nervous energy that kept Carter on edge. Now he was looking at a teenager who almost had a smile on his face. The stubborn don't-mess-with-me-or-I-might-bite-you expression had morphed. Since he'd started working at the campground, Jay's entire demeanor had become so much calmer. Rylie said the campground gave him a safe place to land.

"A little hungry today, dude?" Carter asked, holding back a smile.

"You should really eat something too," a voice said from behind him.

Rylie. An instant longing to go back to the night by the fire when she'd been tucked in close to his side assaulted all his senses at once. He became acutely aware that he had definitely missed her.

Jay had already taken off across the compound, leaving Carter to fend for himself.

Taking a step back to try and break the gravitational pull that seemed to exist between them, he frowned. "How do you know I haven't already eaten? I do know how to cook, you know."

Rylie gave him a little smile. "Because you've been standing here, pretending not to be hungry since you left your cabin."

Carter looked away from her. "I've been up for

hours. I ate before you got up." His stomach growled loudly.

She laughed. "Liar, liar, pants on fire."

"What? Are we seven now?" He scowled. "How would you even know? Maybe I just want second breakfast."

Rylie pointed at his face and winked. "You still have lines on your face from your pillow." She turned and walked away without another word.

It took a lot of self-control not to follow her. Her presence brought warmth and light to his dreary world. It bugged him how much he craved it.

Since Rylie had called him out, Carter gave up the charade that he wasn't absolutely famished and strolled over to the food truck, where he ordered a breakfast garbage plate. He was pretty sure it was enough food to feed him *and* Jay; he was also completely confident that he had plenty of appetite for the entire thing.

Jay had found a seat among the crew. The host, Carlos, was animatedly telling one of his many stories. Jay always hung on every word the man said. To him, Carlos was a hero. Who could blame Jay, though? The man was larger than life to a kid in a small mountain town.

During the week, one of the older, more experienced crew members had taken to showing Jay the finer points of filming and editing a reality television show. The boy's entire personality had shifted since the first night.

Letting him be to enjoy himself, Carter settled on one of the tree-trunk benches set up around the firepit. Balancing his plate on his thigh, he dug into the mound of eggs, home fries, sausage, pancakes, and bacon. It tasted so good; he was fairly certain every bite elicited a moan of pleasure.

When there was nothing left but a few crumbs, Carter seriously considered licking the heavy paper plate clean. As he debated the merits of licking it or refilling it, a shrill shriek filled the air followed immediately by another. The entire crew froze as every single one of them turned in the direction of the campsites.

"Jack!" Rylie yelled as she ran in the direction of the scream. "Come on!"

Dropping his plate on the ground, Carter sprang up and took off running also, forgetting the pain in his knee that still lingered from his fall in the storm. Several steps ahead of Rylie by default, he reached the camping areas where the cast members were gathered on their respective sites.

"What happened?" Carter huffed against the cold air and his burning lungs.

"Is everyone okay?" Rylie asked, coming up beside him, equally out of breath.

Jack followed, along with Jay and the rest of the crew. Carlos brought up the rear.

"What's going on?" Jack asked.

"We heard someone scream!" someone said. "We're missing Kathy, and the other team is missing Abigail."

"*Help! Help me!*" The words echoed up the path from the waterfall area. "*Someone! Please! Come quick!*"

Another cast member let out a sob. "Something terrible has happened. I just know it!"

One of her teammates wrapped an arm around her shoulders, pulling her in for a hug. "After what happened to the crew guy, I'm not going to sit around and wait to find out."

He stormed off in the direction of the waterfall.

Carter ran after him, stopping the man before he could get too far. If something bad had happened, the young man charging down the path definitely didn't need the image in his head. "Stay here. I'll go check it out."

Turning to the rest of the crowd, he said, "I mean

it. All of you stay here until I give the all clear. Got it?"

Jay took a couple steps toward him, but he shook his head. "You, too, buddy. Just wait here." In case something—someone—was there who could hurt him.

As he jogged toward the water, he overheard Jay tell everyone he was the best cop in Staunton and would protect them all.

If only he had as much confidence in his abilities as his young friend did.

Rylie followed him down the path. He let her—not because he wasn't worried about her safety but because if something had happened to one of her cast members, she deserved to be there. Besides, a witness from the network would be good for his own protection.

As the sound of rushing water moved in, he caught sight of a young woman sitting under a tree. Her head rested on her arms that lay across her bent knees. Steady sobs blended with the sound of the water. Her body shook with each new round of emotion.

"Abigail." Rylie passed him to drop to her knees beside the crying woman. "What's wrong? Are you okay?"

Abigail pointed toward the water a few hundred feet away. "It's... it's Kathy!"

Carter walked in the direction the woman had indicated and sucked in a breath. There, face down in the ice-cold water, lay a woman. Her bright red hair floated in a halo around her head. The clothes she wore ballooned slightly, making her body bob on the surface. She had the appearance of someone just floating along, relaxing. Except that she wasn't on her back, and it was about forty degrees outside.

Rylie clapped a hand to her mouth. "Oh no. Please tell me she's not dead."

Carter made his way down the bank, his banged-up knee screaming at him, to try and reach the woman. He finally got ahold of her jeans and pulled the body toward the edge of the water. Feeling for a pulse he knew he'd never find, he dragged her onto the riverbank and started doing CPR. "Call 911," he said to Rylie between compressions. "Tell them there's no pulse, and I've started CPR!"

Even as he gave her rescue breaths and kept up compressions, Carter knew it was too late. He kept going, though, just in case. Stranger things had happened. He couldn't give up.

The familiar sound of sirens eventually cut through the early morning air.

He could hear voices yelling as the sirens suddenly went silent. The woman's heart remained still as he continued breathing and compressions. Two EMTs ran toward him, carrying a jump bag. They both stopped when they saw him.

Still, he kept going.

"Marshall," one of the EMTs said. "How long has she been down?"

He glanced up. Both of the medics had been in the department longer than he'd been a cop. They knew him, his brothers, and his father. They watched him with sadness.

Rylie glanced at her phone. "At least fifteen minutes. It's been that long since we found her."

"Did she have a pulse when you pulled her out?" the older of the two medics, Alan, asked.

Rylie shook her head, but Carter kept going.

Alan squatted so he and Carter were at eye level. "Marshall. Come on, man. She's gone."

"We don't know that. The water is cold. Maybe it protected her or something." He looked at Alan. "Aren't you two going to shock her?"

He knew he sounded desperate. Hell, he felt beyond desperate.

Alan reached over and put his hand on Carter's. "Stop. Let her rest."

Carter froze, suddenly aware of the dozens of pairs of eyes on him. All the desperation melted away as the adrenaline rush suddenly gave out. "I tried."

His words were so quiet, he thought no one had heard him, but he could tell by Rylie's eyes that she had.

Alan offered him a hand. "I know you did, man. I know you did."

Accepting the help, he stood up. Nodding at Alan, Carter climbed up the riverbank. Without another word, he walked away.

There was a hiking trail about three hundred feet down the path past the campsites. Carter needed to be alone, so he headed there.

Jay called after him, but he ignored the boy.

"We really need to get off this mountain!" one of the men bellowed. "This place is cursed!"

Carter just kept walking.

"Are we going to cancel the show?" a woman asked, her words tainted with sobs. "We have to cancel the show."

Carter walked faster.

As the forest swallowed him, the anxious voices and fear-laden faces disappeared, replaced with his own fear and anxiety attempting to swallow his whole being.

RYLIE STOOD up and offered Abigail a hand. "Come on, let's get you out of here. You don't need to watch anymore."

Abigail nodded and accepted her assistance in standing up. As soon as she was steady on her feet, Rylie left Jack to supervise the EMTs and headed back to the camping area. The rest of the cast needed to know what happened.

What Rylie really wanted to do was follow Carter. Her heart told her he'd been facing some pretty big demons just then. Her brain, the part that wanted to keep her job, knew she had to deal with the situation at hand first. She led everyone back to the campsite, an arm around Abigail's waist as they walked. Cast members sobbed as crew people paced around, airing their theories about what had happened to Kathy.

A million different thoughts assaulted her at once. How could she tell the network another person had died? Then there was the immediate problem of needing a new contestant. Should she even get one? And how would they tell the viewers why they had to replace Kathy? They didn't have the time or budget to reshoot the shelter-building and fire-making challenges, so starting over would be unreasonable.

Above all, poor Abigail had discovered the body. Her tear-streaked face held two nearly lifeless eyes. The woman had to be a mess. Rylie walked over to where she now sat and squatted beside her. "I'm so sorry you had to find her like that."

Abigail looked up at Rylie with an anguished face, water still dripping from her chin. "Was she murdered?"

The woman looked like she might shatter if Rylie said yes. Honestly, there was no real way to tell.

Rylie shook her head. "It *looks* like it was just an accident. She probably slipped and fell in. The medical examiner will be able to tell us more, but as far as anyone could see, there was no sign of foul play."

"I think she went there to get water. Same as me. I know we were supposed to be competing against each other, but Kathy is awesome." A fresh round of tears filled her eyes. "I mean, *was* awesome."

Rylie heard Carlos speaking. The man really had a way with people. He'd somehow managed to calm everyone down. A fire was burning at each campsite, and the cast sat around in their respective teams, waiting for direction.

Rylie motioned to both groups to join her on the path between the camps. As everyone gathered around, she took a deep breath to steady her nerves.

Rylie raised her hands to get everyone's attention. "At the moment, it appears to have been accidental, but we need to wait for an investigation to be completed to know for sure. We *think* she slipped trying to get water and fell in. Between the temperature of the water and other factors.... Until we're told otherwise, this is the theory we'll work with."

The sound of sirens in the distance told her police were on the way.

"I totally think this place is cursed," one of the men, a guy named Charlie, said.

"I don't believe in that stuff." Helen, the oldest member of the cast, shook her head. "She just had an accident. The mountains can be a dangerous place, and honestly, Kathy wasn't really the kinda gal to be survivin' in the woods anyway. She was probably tryin' to see her reflection in the water or somethin'. Make sure her hair was perfect. She was always primpin'."

"What a terrible thing to say!" Abigail glared at Helen. "Have a little respect for the dead!"

"Okay, okay. Everyone, please, just calm down." Rylie sent a pleading look to Carlos, who let out a shrill whistle.

The group went silent instantly.

"We're going to take the day off from shooting. Take some time to process and mourn your team-mate. I'm going to go and notify the network and Kathy's next of kin. Carlos and the rest of the crew are going to stay here with you for a bit for support." She turned to the host. "Is that good with you?"

"You betcha, *chica*." He gave her a thumbs-up followed by a little salute. "This is just like the time I was over in Vietnam on a riverboat, comforting the survivors. I got this."

Rylie shook her head as she walked back toward the cabins, wondering exactly what kind of survivors he'd been charged with comforting.

She knew he wasn't nearly old enough to have fought in the Vietnam War. The man had a way of weaving incredible stories, but a part of her didn't doubt his varied experiences, even if they made as much sense as a ladder without any rungs.

The thought of having to call her bosses again to

report another death made her queasy. It felt like Darcy's murder had cast a veil of death over the show.

CHAPTER SIXTEEN

When he finally stopped walking, Carter had gone deep into the woods. Several years ago, on a hike, he'd found an old, abandoned homestead here. It had become his place to go and sit on the edge of the creek. The water ran past a stone structure he assumed was once an icehouse or maybe a cold cellar for food storage. He'd ventured inside once, but all the wooden stairs down into the dirt-walled room were rotted. A fall would mean certain death if he were alone. No one would ever find him.

The place had always given him peace, though. Somewhere to escape the grind of the job—and now, apparently, his campground, which had once provided sanctuary. The only other place that had ever offered any solitude had now become a hotbed of tragedy.

All he'd wanted was a little money to make his dream a reality. There'd been no indication that he was basically selling his soul to the devil in the process.

He couldn't stand to be there when Peters showed up again. The man took literal joy from making Carter feel lousy, and he wasn't about to go through that one more time. Even Vonda seemed to be doubting him, and that hurt.

Carter sat down on the bank of the creek, stretching his legs out in front of him. The knee he'd injured still ached, but stretching it seemed to help. He stayed that way for a long time, listening to the sounds of the woods. Slowly he felt his heart rate return to normal. The anger and agitation he'd been experiencing all week slowly melted away. His shoulders were sore from the psychological weight he'd been carrying around for so long.

The events of *that day* played on a constant repeat in the back of his mind. It'd been a perpetual struggle to ignore it—slog through each day, doing his job and pretending he was okay when okay didn't come close to how he felt. And now he possibly had two accidents that might actually be murders committed on his property on his watch. That did not bode well for his psyche. Or the future of his business.

All around him, leaves of red and gold rustled in the light breeze. Carter leaned back on his elbows and stared up at the canopy. A squirrel sat on a branch, chattering away at him. Otherwise, the wildlife stayed pretty quiet.

Images of the woman floating in the river entered his thoughts. He'd known as soon as he pulled her from the water that she was gone, but something inside him wouldn't let him believe it. A madness drove him as he pumped away at the chest compressions, completely out of control of his own faculties.

A snap in the woods behind the stone house had him sitting straight up in full alert mode. After a few seconds, another louder crack was followed by the distinct shuffle of some leaves. Carter grabbed a nearby rock, jumped to his feet, and made his way toward the structure as quietly but as swiftly as he could.

Slipping inside the entrance of the stone shanty, he listened for any sounds indicating more movement.

Steady cracks and crinkles headed straight toward him had Carter posted up and ready to defend himself. Although it was more likely an animal such as a bear than a human, since no one but him seemed to know about this place, he still stayed ready.

From off in the distance, he heard a voice calling out. "Carter! Where are you, Carter?"

Rylie!

The snapping brush stopped. Carter stayed completely still.

"Carter Marshall! Where did you get off to?" Rylie sounded much closer. The crunching and snapping started up again—this time moving away from his hiding place and back toward the direction of Rylie's voice.

"There's no way he could have gotten this far from camp," he heard her say, which meant she was close.

Then Rylie screamed, the bloodcurdling shriek filling the air and bouncing off the trees. Carter took off as fast as his stiff, now-angry knee would allow. Then he pushed even harder.

After the scream, the woods went deathly silent. He no idea which way to go, so he just kept running, hoping to find something.

The pitchy notes of someone whistling a tune caught his attention. Carter stopped where he stood, listening. The notes were familiar, but he couldn't quite place the song. Afraid to keep going and afraid to not find Rylie in time had him locked in indecision. A fresh flood of adrenaline kicked his heart rate up again as his muscles tensed, and his senses strained for more information.

Inching forward, he stopped after every step and listened. The whistling continued, but there wasn't another hint of Rylie. Two more steps forward, and the whistling stopped. A few seconds later, a light *whoosh* passed by his ear. Carter spun and watched as one of his own arrows from the campground slammed into the trunk of a tree about ten feet ahead of him.

Ducking behind another tree, Carter scanned the area. No more arrows and no other signs of anyone else being in the woods. Careful to stay as hidden as possible, he picked his way through the trees in the direction of where he thought he'd heard Rylie's scream. He strained to hear footsteps behind him or sounds of Rylie in front of him, but the forest remained relatively quiet.

After what felt like forever, he broke out of the trees into a small clearing. He stopped running, gasping at air and praying he'd lost his pursuer.

"Carter!" He heard his name in a harsh whisper.

"Rylie! Where are you?"

Her whisper shouted back as he spun in a slow circle, searching the clearing and the surrounding trees. "Up here." She sounded tired. Or in pain. Or maybe both.

Carter looked up at the trees immediately behind him and sucked in a loud breath, trying to resist laughing. "How on earth did you manage to get up there?"

Rylie hung from a thick branch around ten feet above the ground, her feet dangling as she clutched the branch over her head. The hem of her hoodie had also caught on a knot, so it was pulled up over her face. "Just get me down, please. Then I'll tell you."

Carter took stock of the situation. "Okay. Can you let go, and I'll catch you?"

"My sweatshirt is caught." She sighed. "I'm stuck."

"If you drop down, it'll pull right up over your head." He positioned himself under her, prepared for the force of her weight.

"Yeah, not exactly," Rylie said. "It's hooked under my chin. I might strangle. Otherwise, I would have already let go."

"Oh." Carter scratched his temple, eyeing the

tree. "I think I'm going to have to climb up there and try to get you down. Hang on."

The last time he'd climbed a tree, at the age of twelve, he'd fallen and broken his arm. It took him out of the spring baseball season, which was heart-breaking to him at the time. His fear of heights had also set in around then.

The thought of hauling himself up on those limbs gave him a knot in his gut the size of the entire state of Virginia.

"Hurry, please. My arms are about to give out. Be careful. I saw someone carrying a bow and arrow out in the woods."

Rylie sounded scared. Carter had no choice. "I know. I already had a run-in with him." Praying the person who had fired an arrow at him was long gone, he made up his mind.

"Man up and do this," he murmured, rubbing his suddenly sweaty palms together.

"I'm sorry, but did you just tell me to man up?" Rylie's fear had been replaced with serious anger.

Carter felt the heat rise up his neck and spread over his face in embarrassment. Glad she couldn't see him, he forced a laugh. "I, um, was giving myself a pep talk."

"Oh no," Rylie practically sobbed. "You're afraid of heights, aren't you?"

"Nope. Just trees," he lied as he found a solid branch right below her and hauled himself up. Finally, all the pull-ups he'd done out of frustration paid off on something.

Swinging his leg around so he could sit in the fork formed by the branch and the trunk of the tree, he tried to decide on his next move.

"Carter," Rylie said quietly. "Not to rush you or anything, but my fingers are really slipping."

Nodding like she could see him, he hoped he sounded a whole lot more confident than he felt. "Almost there. Just hang on."

Standing on the branch, he climbed to the next one where Rylie was stuck, praying the entire time that his knee would hold out. Fortunately, he was able to sit on that one and rest at least one foot at a time on the one below for balance.

"You got this," he whispered to himself.

"Please have this," Rylie whispered loudly back at him.

Shimmying forward just enough to be able to unhook her hoodie, he mentally begged the branch to continue to hold them both.

"I'm going to free the material of your sweatshirt.

Can you hang on just a little bit longer so I can get back on the ground?"

"I will try. Please hurry. I don't want to die out here!" This time her voice did crack on a sob.

The image of Rylie lying broken on the ground below them hit him square in the chest.

"Don't worry, sweetheart. I'm not gonna let that happen." With a sudden burst of confidence, he freed the errant clothing from its hang-up, swung down to the lower branch, then dropped to the ground.

Positioning himself once more to cushion her fall, he braced. "Okay, let go. I'm here."

"Are you s—" Rylie's last word was lost in the soft squeal she made when her fingers gave up their grasp on the branch.

She fell straight down into his arms, the force tumbling them both to the forest floor. The air exited his lungs in a *whoosh*, making him feel briefly dizzy. His knee screamed in agony. Rylie exhaled deeply as well. For the second time in as many weeks, she lay on top of him in a pile of leaves.

This time, Carter had his arms wrapped tightly around her, protecting her from falling any farther. At least that was the rationale he provided to himself. In actuality, he liked the feel of her soft curves against his harder frame. It felt like home to him as their heartbeats calmed together.

That had to be a head injury talking. Maybe he smacked his skull on a root or something.

Rylie had her face buried against his chest. He felt a slight movement—in every muscle of his body.

"Did you say something?" He reached up and smoothed her hair down, plucking a twig from her tangled locks. The dizzy feeling had begun to subside as he remembered where they were and how they got here. The person in the woods with the arrows might have returned, just waiting for an opportunity to shoot at him again.

But then, he'd been a perfect target up in the tree, and nothing had happened. Maybe the crazy forest-dwelling killer had left the area.

She turned her head to the side. "Did you actually call me sweetheart?"

Focused on the problem at hand, which was getting them off the ground and safely into the cover of the woods, he barely registered her question. "I don't know. I guess I might have."

Rylie pushed herself up with her arms so they were nearly nose to nose. "You did. It almost sounded like you were scared I might die." Her lips ticked a little at the corners as her green eyes sparkled with humor and a bit of something that looked like attraction.

Carter raised an eyebrow. "I can't have a dead television producer adding to the body count, now can I?"

His words were meant to annoy her enough that she would jump off him and storm away. She didn't move, though—just stared at him, daring him to try to convince her he actually meant what he said.

The urge to kiss her nearly overpowered all the logic and focus telling him to get them out of there and *then* think about how soft her lips would feel. Instead of kissing her, however, he moved his head slightly so he could whisper against her ear.

"Whoever is out here might still be around. We need to get out of this clearing as quickly as possible, just in case." He felt a shiver pass through her, finding himself hoping it was more about his lips next to her ear and less about the life-and-death situation they might be in. "I really think you should consider shutting the production down."

"I know. I feel like we're being watched." She said the words so softly, he almost didn't hear them. "I'm going to roll to the side and stay low. Which way are we going?"

Carter felt the loss of her instantly but forced

himself to ignore it. "The shortest distance to the tree line is behind the tree on the other side. Can you low crawl it?"

"Yes." She slithered away through the brush and grass so smoothly, he'd have sworn she'd done it many times before.

Carter followed closely, his eyes and ears searching everywhere at once. He didn't begin to relax until they were behind the tree line and had walked several hundred feet into the woods. He limped more than walked, but at least they were possibly putting in some distance between them and the perp.

"Do you think we're good now?" Rylie asked quietly while they made their way even deeper into the trees.

"I don't know. I think so." He hadn't seen or heard anything to indicate they were still being followed.

Rylie reached over and took his hand in hers as they walked. "Thank you for getting me down. And we're not shutting down production. I'll get the network to send up security instead."

His first instinct was to pull away. Instead, he squeezed her hand lightly. "I don't agree, but we can discuss it when I get you safely back to the camp. Now that you're down, tell me how you got *up*."

She shrugged. "I saw the man with the bow and arrow. At least, I'm assuming it's a man since they had a hoodie pulled up hiding their face. I climbed up the tree to hide. I'm usually really good at tree climbing. Until I slipped."

"And screamed." Carter squeezed her hand again. "He could have killed you right then."

"I know," she said quietly. "I just kept waiting for an arrow to pierce straight through me."

"Yet you want to keep going with the show." It was a statement, not a question, which elicited a frown from Rylie. In an effort to make her smile again, he chuckled. "You probably scared him half to death with those amazing vocal cords."

"Whatever works, I guess." Rylie stopped walking and looked around. "Are we lost?"

He shook his head. "Nope. I know this mountain like the back of my hand. It's about a mile and a half back to the campground."

"Lead me home, then, brave warrior." Pulling her hand from his, she gripped the crook of his elbow instead.

This felt far more intimate than simple hand-holding. Maybe only to him, though. Rylie seemed far more comfortable with human contact than he was.

Carter shook his head lightly, forcing all the foreign thoughts from his mind. Rylie was there to film a show. He had to find out who was killing people and vandalizing his property. There was absolutely no time for childish crushes. Especially not on the woman who had witnessed the absolute worst failure of his life.

In a torrent of unexpected emotions, he disengaged himself from her hold and took the lead through the woods, ignoring the mixture of disappointment and hurt in those beautiful green eyes now mercifully out of his sight.

CHAPTER SEVENTEEN

Carter Marshall switched from hot to cold faster than the antique water heater at her apartment.

She knew he felt the same reaction she did whenever they touched. Chemistry so volatile couldn't be one-sided. The absolutely engulfing feelings rendered her into putty in his hands. Every time they got close to anything via touch or conversation, he withdrew faster than a turtle into its shell.

His walls were tall and strong, a veritable fortress around his heart. Rylie had a show to finish. If only people would stop turning up dead, maybe she'd be able to wrap up the show and set to work unwrapping Carter's heart.

Now she sounded like a cheesy romance-novel heroine.

"Carter?"

"Yeah?" He didn't even look back at her.

"I'm sorry people from my show keep dying." The words sounded so dumb to her own ears; she could only imagine how they sounded to him.

"Are you the one killing them?" he asked, moving a branch out of the way for them to get past it.

"Of course not!"

He shrugged. "Then you have nothing to apologize for."

Rylie followed him past the branch. "I saw you after the medics arrived. You went into the woods. I was worried you were going to do something rash."

Carter stopped walking but didn't turn around. "Is that why you came out here? You thought I was going to hurt myself?"

She took a step closer and placed a hand on his shoulder. She felt him tense immediately. "I was a little worried, yes. I could see how incredibly upset you were."

"You could have died out here!" Stepping forward, away from her touch, Carter shrugged again. "I'm getting used to failing. I'm not going to hurt myself. I just needed some time alone."

He started walking again. Rylie got the distinct feeling that there would be no more conversation. Warm, friendly Carter had just been banished by guilt-laden, sad, and angry Carter.

The rest of the trek back to the campground was eerily quiet. Carter didn't say another word, and Rylie suspected it was best she not talk either. By the time they stepped from the trees into the clearing by the waterfall, the place was empty. Aside from some trampled grass and a mass of muddy footprints by the water, there was no sign of the terrible thing that happened there earlier.

"Rylie!" Jack's voice broke the silence. "Where have you been? Are you okay? I've been worried sick! You don't need to be wandering the woods alone right now."

She gestured to Carter. "I wasn't alone. At least not most of the time."

Carter walked off, his gait increasing despite the pronounced limp that had set in as soon as he'd spotted Jack.

"The medical examiner called. It looks like Kathy took a hit to the head before she drowned." Jack tried to link arms with her, but she pulled away.

"They did an autopsy already?" She'd expected it to take a couple of days like Mikey's had.

Jack shook his head, reaching for her again, but she pretended not to notice and bent over to adjust her boot.

"Just a preliminary finding. Could have been self-inflicted as she fell. Said she'd know more in a couple of days."

They were almost to the cabins. All Rylie wanted to do was take some ibuprofen and lie down.

"How are the cast and crew?" she asked, eyeing the door to her cabin. "Everyone good?"

Jack held out his hands, palms facing up. "As good as can be expected. The boss said no replacement for Kathy. We're to work her accident into the show and make it super emotional. It'll raise the ratings."

She stopped and looked at him in complete disbelief. "Are you serious? That was his response—to use her death for ratings?"

Jack shrugged. "That's how it works in television."

"Her family will never agree to that." Rylie threw her hands in the air out of frustration. "I am so over this show and everything about it. Maybe we *should* cancel filming."

She stomped off, leaving a red-faced Jack with his mouth hanging open. With absolutely no interest in what he would have said anyway, she yanked open her cabin door, stepped inside, and slammed it so hard, it hurt in her chest.

Between Carter and Jack, if she never talked to another man again, it might be too freaking soon. The last thing she wanted was to cancel the show, but Carter wasn't wrong about the danger. Honestly, it surprised her that the local police hadn't already insisted.

After pulling off the stupid sweatshirt that had nearly killed her and kicking off her boots, Rylie dropped onto the narrow cot and flung her arm over her eyes.

"Ugh. I forgot the pain medicine for this damn headache." She got up, went into the tiny bathroom, and grabbed the pills. She popped two with almost an entire bottle of water she'd found in the mini fridge, then returned to her tiny bed and fell asleep.

THE SUNSET DUSTING the top of the trees with pinks and purples was the perfect setting for the last bonfire meeting of the second week of filming. Contrary to her expectations, things had gone incredibly smoothly since Kathy's accident. The online news outlets had started reporting on the mysterious deaths at the Blue Ridge Mountains Campground and Survival School, but instead of tanking her show, it seemed to be building serious anticipation for the first episode due out after the new year.

If they could just finish off one more week, she'd be able to go back to the city and forget about the campground and its infuriating owner. After he saved her from the tree, she'd expected they might spend more time together.

She couldn't have been more wrong.

Carter had been cordial, but just like after their night by the campfire, he'd grown distant. Their relationship was now less exciting than the one she had with her dentist. Not that it really resembled a dentist's visit. Rylie really hated going to the dentist.

Pushing away thoughts of the man who shouldn't be taking up any real estate in her head anyway, she tried to focus on their last Friday night campfire. The cast had been a bit subdued the first couple of days after Kathy drowned, but it didn't take long to reignite the competition among the rookie survivalists. By midweek, they would be done filming and a winning team decided. She'd get off this mountain soon and never have to deal with him again.

"Hey there, little lady." Carlos walked over to the log she sat on by the firepit and settled down beside her. He always sat there during the campfire meetings.

"Hey, Carlos. You ready for the last week of filming?"

He pulled his cowboy hat off and ran his fingers through his hair. "Well, you know, this has been a total hoot and a holler, but I'm looking forward to getting home to my woman."

"I know what you mean." Rylie rested her elbows on her knees and leaned forward to study the fire. "I think it might be nice to get back to the city."

"You sure about that?" he asked, stretching his long legs out in front of him. The firelight glinted on the high-shine polish of his boots.

Rylie looked at him with confusion. "Why wouldn't I be?"

He shrugged nonchalantly. "Going there means leaving here, and I think maybe you like it here. Like certain *people* here."

Her face suddenly felt warm, and it wasn't from the fire. "What exactly do you mean?"

"I've noticed the way you look at our host when he's around. But more importantly, it's obvious in the way he looks at you. Pretty sure he's gonna be a sad fella when you leave."

"I don't know what you're talking about." She picked up a stick and began dragging it through the sand. "He barely speaks to me."

Carlos raised an eyebrow at her. "It's what he *doesn't* say, darlin', that you should be paying attention to. The boy carries a heavy load. It weighs him down like a twelve-foot gator on his shoulders. But when you're around, the gator shrinks to maybe five feet."

Rylie laughed. "That's the most ridiculous analogy I've ever heard."

He looked hurt. "Why? There's a huge difference in the size of a twelve-footer and a five-footer. I wrestled them both in the bayou, and let me tell you, that little guy was squirrely!"

She laughed again but had no chance to say anything else as the cast members began to trickle in.

"Rylie!" Jay jogged over to where she sat. "Can I hang around and help the camera guys again tonight?"

The change in Jay in just the past two weeks was a complete metamorphosis. Between her caterers and Carter's heavy home cooking, he'd gained some solid weight and lost that hollowed, gaunt look.

There was a sparkle in his eye and a spring in his step. He'd lost the huge chip on his shoulder and adjusted his attitude to something positive. She loved everything about the changes and would totally take him home with her to California if she could.

His angry drunk of a father would probably sign him over to her, too, just to be rid of the responsibility.

Jay stood in front of her, looking at her pleadingly. Rylie couldn't help but smile. "Sure thing, buddy. You've been a great help the past two weeks."

"You know what you need, dude?" Carlos asked Jay.

"What?" The boy lit up whenever the show host talked to him. She was fairly certain his attention had been at least partly responsible for Jay's change in personality.

"A cowboy hat." He pointed toward his cabin. "Run on back to my digs and grab the one off the hook by the door. You can't be livin' up here in God's country without a proper hat. It's yours if you want it."

"Seriously?" The boy's face filled with excitement. "I never thought about being a cowboy."

Carlos laughed. "Seriously. Go on now and grab

it. The hat won't make the man—the man makes the hat. Always remember that, boy."

"Oh, man. Thank you!" Jay turned and ran off toward the cabin, stopping to look back. "I promise to always remember."

"We should get this thing started." Rylie stood up on the tree-trunk bench. "Can I get you all to pay attention over here, please? Our host is going to start the meeting. Remember, cameras are rolling as soon as I get down from here."

She stepped down as promised and disappeared from the view of the cameras.

Carlos stood up and tipped his hat to the cast. "Congratulations to y'all for making it this far. The competition has been tight. Both groups have nearly the same number of points accumulated. This last week is going to take things to a new level."

Her host always held the contestants' attention. Something in the way he spoke captured them. Rylie's job was done for a bit.

Off in the distance, she spotted Carter leaning against a tree. The dark blue flannel shirt he wore probably made his blue eyes even more brilliant than they normally were. She'd like to get close enough to find out. His arms were crossed over his chest, and he wore a dark-colored knit cap. The whole picture belonged on the cover of an outdoorsman or camping magazine.

Her heart did a little flutter thing in her chest as she started moving in his direction. Carter's eyes never left her as she walked toward him. They'd been dancing around each other long enough, and she was exhausted with the game. With only one week left, it was time to find out if all the feelings she'd been having about him were mutual.

She suspected they were. Carlos said they were, and he had a talent for reading people, it seemed. Rylie also knew with 100 percent certainty that Carter had been completely driven by Darcy's death. The weight of that day never seemed to leave him.

Carter continued to watch her as she walked straight toward him. As the distance between them lessened, she saw the question in his eyes shift to something that maybe resembled desire.

Without a word, Rylie grabbed him by the hand and pulled him along with her to a dark area away from the cast and crew. Carter didn't resist. Maybe he knew what was coming, or perhaps he didn't have a clue. It definitely didn't matter. Rylie was a woman on a mission.

Placing her hands on his chest, she backed him up against a tree, stood on tiptoe, and kissed him.

The moment their lips met, Rylie knew. This was exactly the right thing to do. She slid her hands up the soft flannel of his shirt and wove her fingers into the hair at the back of his head. Carter hesitated briefly, then pulled her in tight against his chest, anchoring her with his arms wrapped around her lower back.

The explosion of light and chemistry everyone always talked about was real. Rylie had read about it in books, seen it in movies, but she'd never actually believed it to exist. The moment he pulled her in close, she knew her world had completely changed.

Carter's heart raced. She felt every heartbeat against her own chest. His hands slid down to her waist, gripping her hips and holding her in place. Time seemed to stand still as they allowed themselves to feel something absolutely amazing.

Carter pulled away first, resting his chin against her hair, but he didn't let go of her.

"What was that for?" He sounded as breathless as she felt.

Rylie lay her head on his chest, listening to the sound of his heart. "I'm not sure, to be honest." She pulled back and looked up at him. Carter still hadn't let her go, which was totally okay in her book. "It just felt like the right thing to do."

He didn't say anything at first. His eyes said plenty, though, as he leaned in for another kiss. His lips had barely grazed hers when Jay appeared.

"Carter! Look at this hat Carlos gave me!" The boy froze, mouth hanging open as he realized what he'd interrupted. "Oh, man, I'm so sorry. It's about time, though! I'm gonna go help with the cameras!"

He trotted off, practically skipping with delight.

Carter let go of Rylie—something her body hated instantly. She laughed. "That boy has lousy timing."

"Yeah, he does." Carter gazed down at her with a rare genuine smile that reached his eyes. "He's really changed a lot, hasn't he?"

She smiled back and nodded. "He has. It's been amazing to see him evolve so much. I bet he won't be getting into any more trouble going forward."

"I'm sorry I've been distant this week. I had a lot going on with the cops and the investigations. They still haven't found the crazed archer out in the woods." Carter made a sweeping motion to indicate the entire campground. "You know how it is—they probably never will. We're lucky they didn't shut down the show."

She shrugged and smiled. "They agreed to let it go on when my boss offered to pay the overtime to have cops on-site twenty-four hours a day for security."

Carter frowned, obviously unhappy with that arrangement. "Yeah, I know."

Not to be deterred, Rylie laced her fingers with his. "I know you've been avoiding me. Just like you did after we talked by the fire. I really just don't understand why."

"It's complicated." He tried to let go of her hand, but she placed her other hand over their entwined ones. "I like you. Which in itself is hard enough for me to work my broken mind around. I don't want to burden you with... well, me."

"Not really all that complicated, actually. I think I understand pretty well. Somewhere along the way, you convinced yourself you aren't worthy of love and are doomed to live the life of a hermit on the top of a mountain. Then I came along and upset all your plans." She smiled up at him.

He reached up and traced the line of her jaw. "You certainly have caused an upset." Carter sighed. "I just can't... do this. You deserve so much more than I have to offer. I'm an old man, set in my ways."

Rylie laughed. "We're the same age."

He raised an eyebrow. "We are not. We can't be."

She nodded. "Actually, you're a couple of years older than me. That's probably why you don't remember."

He looked confused. "I told you I remembered you from that night."

She shook her head. "Not from the show. From high school."

Carter frowned, obviously confused. "I thought I pretty much knew everyone from our school."

Rylie took a deep breath to calm her nerves. Thinking about that night always made her shaky, even after the better part of two decades. "I was a freshman when you were a senior. I played the flute in the marching band. One night after a game... two older guys...."

She saw the exact moment he realized who she was. The same anger she'd seen in his eyes as he pulled those guys off her returned with a vengeance.

"That was you?" He paced a couple of steps. "I'm sorry. I had no idea."

Rylie touched his arm. "It was a long time ago. I was a young girl. I didn't expect you to remember me the way I remembered you. You saved my life. If you hadn't shown up when you did, things would have gone very, very wrong. I would have become a very different person."

He nodded, thoughtfully. "Rylie Christianson. Now I know why that name seemed so familiar when you called the first time. I never would have imagined someone from Staunton making it to Los Angeles. At least now I understand why you did what you did for me."

"How could I not? I know you didn't remember me, but I never forgot the handsome Marshall brother who saved me."

He frowned. "Anyone would have done the same. All I did was scare them off."

"Actually, not anyone would have, but you did. As for Cali, my parents relocated us out there my junior year when my grandmother became ill. I don't have some making-it-big story. I just happened to answer an ad in a paper for an assistant to an assistant at the network."

"I'm glad everything turned out well for you." He sighed. "Things didn't go quite as well here, as you can see. The shooting that day, the deaths here—it's all just too much. I was a failure as a cop, again as a business owner, and quite possibly as a human too."

"Carter Marshall, none of this has anything to do with you at all!" She planted her hands on her hips and glared up at him. "It's time you got your head out of your ass and realized that sometimes bad things just happen. Even to good people. *Especially* to good people. You can't carry the weight of everything all the time."

They stood there, each daring the other to speak and neither willing to break the strained silence.

Finally, Carter spoke. "I screwed up with your boss. I should have been able to save her."

She placed her hands on his chest. His entire being was tense. "You saved me once when we were kids, even if you don't remember it. Twice if you count the whack to the head in the barn. Three times if we're counting the tree today—and I definitely am. You were in pain and hate tree climbing, yet you did it anyway. You're 100 percent a hero. It's in everything you are. You've just set the bar for yourself so incredibly high that you'll never be able to meet your own expectations. You need to stop trying to be everything to everyone and just be the amazing man you already are. Look what you've done for Jay. His entire life changed because of you. He walks around with his head held high now."

Carter grasped her wrists lightly and gently pushed her away. "I just can't be what you need. No matter how much I'd like to be. I've got to set things right with the universe before I can begin to even think about what I want."

He started to walk away but stopped when Rylie spoke. "It's a damn shame. Cloaked in all that guilt and self-sacrifice is a lonely existence. For the record, you are the only one who holds you responsible for Darcy's death."

"What about the others? This is my property. I'm responsible for everything that happens here."

She scoffed, sarcasm heavy in her next words. "That's right, Carter Marshall. It's all your fault. Go on now, you better get moving. You're late for your self-pity party."

Rylie started to storm off but froze when she heard Jay's panicked voice.

"Hey! Don't do that!" he called out from somewhere in the dark.

A chorus of screams sounded from the firepit area.

"Stop!" Jay cried out. "Miss Rylie! Carter! Help!"

Carter took off at top speed toward the campfire.

"You know, I always hated archery." The words echoed over the now-silent crowd. Shock and pain filled Carlos's dark eyes as he gripped the fiberglass rod sticking from his chest and pulled it out. He crumpled to the ground with a thud. "It's too dangerous for...."

The arrow, just like all the others, appeared to be from the supply barn.

"No!" Rylie sobbed, running around the agitated crowd. She dropped to her knees beside the dead man. "Carlos! Mr. Flores! Please! Don't be dead!"

She knew that the moment the arrow had pierced his chest, he was gone.

Carter came up behind her and scooped her off the ground. "You can't touch the body," he said against her ear so only she could hear. "There might be evidence."

She buried her face in his neck, though the feeling of his arms holding her offered no comfort.

He set her gently on her feet and made sure she was steady before letting go. "I have to find Jay. Call 911 and send everyone to the dining hall. Don't let them go anywhere until we find the person responsible for this."

Rylie nodded as he disappeared. After instructing her camera crew to herd the cast to the dining hall, she pulled out her cell phone and dialed the emergency number.

An older-sounding woman answered, snapping

some gum as she spoke. "911. What's your emergency?"

Rylie took a deep breath. "I think there's been a murder at the Blue Ridge Mountains Campground and Survival School."

"Oh my Lord. Is Carter okay?" The dispatcher went from all business to complete worry and fear. "If I have to call his mama—"

"He's fine. But my show host has been shot in the chest with an arrow." Carlos lay at her feet, his open eyes no longer seeing. Rylie shivered, fighting back a fresh round of tears. The adrenaline had her shaking as she tried to hold her phone to her ear.

"Police, EMS, and the medical examiner are on the way. Are you or is anyone else injured, dear?"

"N-No. Everyone's just really shaken up."

"Is Carter with you?" the woman asked.

She shook her head before remembering that the dispatcher couldn't see her. "No. He's off looking for Jay—a teen who helps us out here on the weekends. He lives in town, and we can't find him."

"Do you think he did this?" Keyboard keys clicked wildly through the phone.

"Nope. Not at all. But I think he might have seen who did."

"Are you in a safe place?" More clicking. The sound had really started to get on her nerves.

"As safe as anywhere on a mountain at a camp-ground in the dark with a killer on the loose can be," Rylie replied, forgetting sarcasm wouldn't help the situation.

"Help is on the way. Please don't let anyone near the body." The line went dead.

Emergency operators weren't supposed to just drop a call like that, were they?

Absolutely nothing made sense anymore.

CHAPTER EIGHTEEN

CARTER BOUNDED THROUGH THE TREES, following the crashing sounds of someone else running ahead of him.

Every now and then, he'd hear Jay calling out to the person he pursued. Hoping he'd catch up with Jay before the teen caught up with a possible murderer, Carter picked up his speed. The toe of his boot hooked a raised tree root, sending him flying toward the ground—only the ground sloped away as he rolled head over heels down into a ravine. At some point, his body slammed against some brush and came to a rest.

With the air forced from his lungs, Carter blacked out. For how long, he didn't know. It could have been a minute, or it could have been an hour

271

when his eyes finally opened to the dark forest. Every inch of his body hurt. Tentatively stretching his arms and legs, he checked for injury. Everything seemed to mostly be okay, aside from a solid headache and being really sore. Carter worked his way up to a sitting position.

His vision swam but eventually settled as he sat there, trying to remember how he'd gotten three feet from an ice-cold stream at the bottom of a ravine. Then he remembered Jay.

He jumped to his feet way too quickly, and he gripped a nearby tree for support. He had to find Jay. There was a killer on the mountain, and the boy was no doubt in danger.

As he stood there, waiting to see if balance was still a thing, a light shone down from above him. "Carter? Is that you?"

Jay. Thank the Lord.

Carter gave a little wave. "Yeah, buddy, it's me. Are you okay?"

"I'm fine, but he got away." Jay exhaled heavily. "I got so close. Are *you* okay?"

Carter let go of the tree to find out the world had finally stopped spinning, and besides some aches and pains, he seemed to be relatively fine. Enough to get himself back to camp anyway. "I'm good, dude. Stay there, and I'll come to you. No more chasing possible murderers."

"Be careful. I don't want anything to happen to you." Jay sounded like a scared little boy.

"Nothing's gonna happen to me, dude. I'm tough as nails. I promise. It just might take me a minute." Carter stifled a groan as he began the climb back up the ravine.

When he finally made it to the top, Jay extended his hand to him to help him the last bit of the way.

Carter smiled at the effort but knew there was no way the teen could support his weight as he accepted his hand.

Once he'd crested the top, he leaned against a tree and took several deep breaths with Jay watching him, still worried.

"It was him." Jay shifted his weight and ran his fingers through his hair.

Carter straightened up. "It was who, Jay?"

"The guy with the bow and arrow. It was the cameraman who likes to hang around Miss Rylie."

"Are you saying Jack killed the show host?" Carter's fists clenched as he realized the man hadn't been anywhere around all day.

Jay nodded. "I saw him as I headed back to the

campfire to show Mr. Carlos the hat. He was in the trees by the cabin that burned down."

"And you thought it was a good idea to chase after him?"

He looked at the ground. "I wanted to stop him from shooting. I was too late, though. So I thought if I could keep an eye on him until you heard me call for help, we'd be able to catch him."

Carter placed his hands on the boy's shoulders and looked him in the eyes. "Are you absolutely certain that the man you saw was Jack?"

Jay nodded. "I'm sure."

"We need to get back to the campground." Carter started making his way through the woods.

Jay followed him cautiously. "I thought we were lost."

"I know this mountain very well. Just stay close in case the killer is still out here."

A few minutes later, they broke out of the trees and into the clearing where the campground began. Blue and red lights flashed all over the parking area. Uniformed officers meandered around the space and stood sentinel at the doors to the dining hall.

"Come on." He motioned to Jay to follow him to the campfire area, where he expected to find Rylie with the body and the crime scene people.

"Marshal!" Vonda greeted him first. "The TV gal says you were with her, working on some paperwork when this happened. Guess you're in the clear. Right, Peters?"

Detective Peters scowled. "Guess so. What kind of paperwork were you doing on a weekend, though?"

Squaring up to the detective, he glared at him. "What is your actual issue with me, Peters? Did I steal your lunch money or something?"

Peters met his glare. "I'm just tired of the entire department treating you Marshalls like you're royalty or something because your old man was on the job since God himself was a child."

Carter held his stare. "You do realize I'm not a cop anymore, right? I'm no longer a threat to your ego."

Peters opened his mouth to reply, but someone called his name. When the man turned away, Carter walked off. He'd never understand the detective's dislike of him. He had better things to worry about anyway.

"Vonda, do you know where Rylie went?"

She pointed at the medical examiner and her assistant. "She was right there a few minutes ago. Such a shame about the host dude. He was a pretty funny guy. I got to talk to him the last time we were out here."

"Yeah. He was definitely okay. You sure she was here?" Carter scanned the crowd once more.

Vonda shrugged and went back to taking photos. "Maybe nature called. It happens to actual humans, you know."

"Don't go anywhere, Marshall!" Peters called out. "We've got this place on lockdown. No one in or out."

He gave Peters a halfhearted salute that may have included his middle finger.

"Jay, go to the dining hall and stay with the cast and crew. I want you safe while I look for Rylie."

"Maybe Miss Rylie went there too. I'll go check." He started to jog off, but Carter stopped him.

"If she's there, send me a text so I know. I'll be out here talking to a couple of the officers. You got your phone on you with my number in it still?"

Jay nodded and patted the front right pocket of his jeans. "Got it. Be careful, okay?"

"Always. Now get on over there."

Carter watched until Jay was safely inside the dining hall building before asking around if anyone had seen Rylie. None of the uniformed officers remembered talking to her. A couple minutes later, his phone vibrated.

> Jay: Miss Rylie not here. Worried.

> Carter: Okay. You stay put inside there. I'm going to look around.

> Jay: K. Don't get dead.

> Carter: I'll do my best, buddy.

No Jack and no Rylie. They had to be together— it was the only thing that made sense. Which meant Rylie was now in danger, if Jay was right about what he'd seen.

No panicking. Not until he was sure.

Carter jogged over to her cabin and knocked. "Rylie! You in there?"

He tried the knob. It turned. Pushing the door open, he stuck his head through the opening. "Rylie?"

He stepped inside and did a quick search, but the place was empty. He ran back outside and looked around. Over on the side of the cabin, he caught sight of something lying on the ground.

Rylie's hat. The one with the little mouse ears on it she'd been wearing the past few days.

A little farther away, almost outside the illumination of the campground lights, lay a glove. The second glove sat on the ground at the edge of the tree line.

She'd left him a trail of cheese. Smart woman.

Peters appeared around the side of the cabin. "Hey, Marshall! Where you going? I told you we're on lockdown!"

"Back off, dude. Rylie's missing. I have to find her." Carter turned and walked into the woods.

"You think the killer got her?" Peters asked, following him into the trees.

"He must have. He's got a thing for her, and I think he was jealous of her friendship with the host. I bet he wanted to create chaos so he could slip away with Rylie and no one would notice until it was too late." He ripped at brush and pushed branches aside.

"Wait." Peters stopped walking, grabbing Carter on the shoulder. "You know who it is? Why the hell didn't you just say that?"

"I didn't know. Not at first. Jay says he saw the cameraman, Jack, with the bow and arrow." Carter pulled his shoulder out of the other man's grasp and started moving again. "And now I think I know where they are."

"Tell me where. I'll get some of the guys and go

after her." Peters tried to grab him again, but Carter pushed ahead.

"Forget that. I'm going now. I can't let anything happen to her. Not like—" He let the sentence fade out as his focus returned to the mission. "You need to protect the rest of the cast and crew. They could all be in danger."

Saving Rylie was his only priority in that moment.

He had to find her before he was too late. Again. Peters and the others could protect everyone else.

Peters put his hand back on Carter's shoulder and squeezed just right in the place that stopped him in his tracks.

"Get your hand off me, Peters."

"Sorry, man, but you aren't going anywhere. We can't risk anyone else getting hurt." He turned Carter around and walked back out of the woods. Peters motioned to a small group of uniformed officers milling around the crime scene. "Take Marshall to the dining hall. He's a possible target of the killer. We need him protected and out of sight of the woods."

"No!" Carter jerked away from Peters, but he was too late. The officers surrounded him and forced him to walk to the dining hall. "You have to let me go! He's going to kill her. I have to stop him!"

"If you tell me *where* to go, I can get a party together and start a search. Your cooperation will let us find her all that much more quickly." Peters walked close but didn't try to touch him again.

Good choice if he valued the full use of his shooting hand.

"There's an old, abandoned building on the bank of a creek. I was there earlier, and I think Jack was too. It's so deep in, I don't know how he found it at all."

"So, you think he found this place again—in the dark?" Peters sounded doubtful.

"I *know* he did." Carter felt the panic begin to build as he imagined all the things Jack could be doing to Rylie in the old building. His pulse raced, and a light sheen of perspiration covered his forehead. He *had* to figure out a way to get to her. There was no way Peters and a team of guys unfamiliar with the mountain would find her in time. Policy dictated procedures to follow in an armed hostage situation. Peters had always been a policy guy.

Procedures Carter knew all too well. They even worked sometimes. But not in the worst, most dangerous domestic-type situations, and that was exactly what was happening.

Jack wanted Rylie, and he'd killed to get her.

"Tell me where, and we'll go get her. I promise we'll bring her back safe."

Peters sounded so confident that Carter almost preemptively felt bad for him, knowing he'd fail to keep his promise. They'd reached the dining hall entrance. In a split second, he had a plan.

"I don't have coordinates or anything. Head into the woods where you found me and push northeast. Eventually, you'll find a decent-sized creek. Follow it to a small clearing, maybe a mile or two in, until you find a shed-sized shanty made of cobblestone." Carter broke free of the officers surrounding him and pulled open the door to the building. "Don't wait too long to go after her. He's not going to drag this out. I feel it in my gut."

Carter let the door slam behind him, ignoring anything else Peters might have tried to say to him. Instead, he beelined to the office, yanked open the safe where he kept his gun, and pulled it out. He slipped it into the waistband of his jeans, then grabbed a flashlight from the top of the file cabinet and ran out through the kitchen to the back door.

Rounding the corner where the prep counter was, he caught sight of an officer posted at the back exit. He shoved a pile of stainless steel prep pans off the counter and watched the officer as they fell to the tile floor with a tumultuous crash.

As predicted, the guard officer leaped toward the sound of the cookware, and Carter ran out the back door of the building. He didn't stop running until he was able to disappear into the tree line.

"Hey! Come back here!" someone, probably the officer he'd just duped, yelled into the night as he put more and more distance between them.

He'd given Peters slightly distorted directions. The site wasn't exactly northeast. They'd find it eventually. He just needed to buy himself some time to get to Rylie first.

Carter cut to the north and started making his way through the trees and brush to where he was certain he'd find Rylie.

So much seemed to ride on rescuing her. Much more than just being the hero. Getting her out of there alive would barely begin to mend the wound he nursed. The rogue rescue would likely get him arrested. He just didn't care anymore. The thought of Rylie in danger made his heart pound and his stomach clench with fear. All that mattered was getting to her.

When she'd kissed him earlier in the evening, Carter had run the gamut of emotions. From fear to anger at himself to holy hell, he wanted to kiss her for the rest of his life.

His emotions were so stunted and dull, though, that he knew he could never give her what she wanted in a relationship. Rylie had fire and passion. Carter just didn't anymore. Life, and the job, had seen to that when he failed at the one thing he'd promised to do— protect the innocent. That one event in time had set his future on an undeniable course of self-loathing.

He wasn't anywhere near an expert on love but was absolutely positive his brittle, shriveled heart would just cause her pain—no matter how much he thought he might be falling for her.

He couldn't give her the love she deserved, but he sure as hell could give her the opportunity to find it out there eventually.

Rylie was young—okay, not as young as he'd thought—and fresh and full of life. He could never get enough of being around her or kissing her, but his darkness would overtake her light sooner rather than later, and she just deserved so much more.

Provided Jack hadn't already extinguished that light for her.

The image of Rylie suffering made his feet move faster. He just needed to find her alive. That was all. He could live a lifetime alone on his mountain as long he knew she was okay. There'd be no way he'd survive if he didn't get to her in time.

CHAPTER NINETEEN

RYLIE FELT SOMETHING RUN OVER THE TOP OF her boot and prayed it wasn't a rat. It was, though—she was sure of it. Feigning ignorance to the situation helped keep the panic at bay. Her captor had covered her eyes and tied her hands behind her back once they'd gotten out of sight of everyone at the campground. Ambushing her as she headed back to her cabin to grab her iPad, he'd clapped a hand over her mouth. His hot breath stank of garlic and beer as he whispered, "Don't scream or fight or I'll cut you." Rylie had done as she was told. Unfortunately, she hadn't gotten a single chance to get a look at him with the knife pressed to her lower spine.

He'd practically dragged her through the woods

to this place. It felt like they'd walked forever to get here, and once they had, he'd pretty much shoved her down some rickety, rotted wood steps. Her foot had gone through one of the boards, sending her flying forward and landing on damp, musty-smelling dirt.

Without her hands free to break her fall, she'd tried hard to roll through the landing. The hard hit had most likely broken her right collarbone and dislocated her shoulder, based on the agonizing pain coursing through her at the moment.

The space was icy cold. Rylie knew she'd be losing body heat fast. If someone didn't find her soon....

Nope. Not thinking about that.

Focus, girl.

There had to be a way to get free. An attempt to loosen the zip tie around her wrists resulted in pain shooting through her with an intensity that nearly made her black out.

A scream she tried hard to suppress escaped, echoing through the room she sat in. Rylie froze, expecting her captor to say or do something. When nothing happened, she sucked in a breath, bit down hard on her lip, and tried again.

The zip tie refused to budge.

Confident she was alone, Rylie started talking to herself out loud. "Okay, lady, that isn't going to work."

Hearing her own voice gave her a little boost that allowed her to try to slide her arms under herself and bring them from behind to the front. Breathing and crying through the pain, she eventually managed to shift enough to bring her hands under her legs and feet in front of her. Rylie sat covered in a cold sweat from the agonizing pain.

Letting herself recover just enough to stop sobbing, she lifted her uninjured arm, which dragged the injured one with it, and pushed the blindfold from her eyes. Leaning back against an ice-cold rock wall, she concentrated on not hyperventilating over the agony in her shoulder.

As she contemplated her next move—climbing those dilapidated steps that were much higher than she'd thought—a light shone down from above, blinding her.

"Well, look at you," a man—presumably her captor—said from behind the light. His voice had a slight familiarity to it, but not enough for her to pinpoint his identity. "Planning an escape? Don't bother. You're not goin' anywhere."

The sound of running water caught her attention. Only she didn't think it was water. Some of the cool liquid splashed down the stairs and onto her jacket.

There was no mistaking the familiar, nauseating scent of gasoline.

Panic overtook her as she forced herself to her feet. "Please! Don't do this. I'll give you whatever you want."

"Oh, you kinda already have, sweetheart." His laughter was vile.

Rylie suddenly knew exactly who she was talking to. "Mason?"

"Ding, ding, ding! We have a winner!"

She could feel the pure evil pouring off him as he cackled at his own joke.

"How did you get out of prison?" Maybe if she could keep him talking, he wouldn't light a match, and she'd have more time to try to figure a way out of the giant mess she was in.

"It's amazing how gullible those corrections officers can be. You'd think after a career in a maximum-security facility, they wouldn't fall for the most basic fake-a-heart-attack ploy. The mob went wild when guards rushed in." He guffawed again, obviously very proud of whatever he did to escape. "The cafeteria became total chaos. I was able to slip out. I planned it all perfectly. A delivery truck was offloading to the kitchen. I simply hitched a ride by hiding inside it and jumped out at their next stop. Honestly, I never expected to get away with it, yet here we are."

He laughed again—an evil, cunning sound that made her skin crawl along with every other emotion she felt.

The room was starting to fill with noxious fumes, making it difficult to think straight. *Please let someone find me.* Rylie slowly slid herself away from the gasoline-soaked stairs. "You're free. So, why come back here?"

"Duh. Revenge." Mason popped open a Zippo lighter and lit a flame.

"What have I ever done to you?" The panic suddenly switched to anger and indignation. "Did you kill Mikey and Carlos Flores too? Oh God! Did you kill Kathy?"

He turned the light on himself, in which she saw him shrug and flip the lighter on again. "Collateral damage. I had to make sure suspicion was averted. The woman *was* an accident that ended up serving my purpose. She saw me and startled. Hit her head on the way into the water."

Rylie had tears pouring down her face at this point as she continued to slowly move farther into the dark and away from the serial killer with the lighter. "Those people had families. People who loved them."

Mason shrugged. "Yeah, well, that's the very definition of collateral damage. Did you like what I did to your car? The owl was a nice touch, wasn't it?"

"That was you? It was a rental, you sociopath!" Her head pounded, threatening to explode at any moment.

"The network has insurance. Not so sure about your boyfriend, though. The cabin went up like kindling." Mason snapped his fingers and made a "Poof" sound.

"You got out! You could have disappeared for good."

His face looked distorted in the beam of the flashlight. "How could I miss watching my twin brother follow you around like a lovesick puppy dog and get the chance to set him up for murder *before* I disappeared? Nope. I wouldn't have missed any of this for all the money in the world. And now, thanks to all my careful planning, everyone will think he killed you and those men who liked you in a jealous rage."

The gas fumes had begun to go to her brain. Mason's image swam as he waved the flame of his lighter in the air in front of him. His words barely made any sense.

"You're completely deranged! They will never believe it was Jack. I don't know how you managed to not get caught yet, but the cops *will* find you. Especially after this. Jack has been off-site all night. He has an alibi!"

Rylie heard the slur in her words and started to panic again. She'd pass out in just a few minutes.

There was a long pause, as though Mason hadn't actually thought all of this through.

Suddenly, something occurred to her.

"You've been here the whole time, haven't you? That was you staying in the barn." She coughed, fighting off the dizziness that wanted to take her over.

"Jack has always been everyone's favorite. Do you have any idea what it's like growing up in the shadow of your twin brother? The good son. The smart twin. The only thing I ever had that was better was Darcy, and he messed that up for me too!"

Rylie's head rolled to the side. "How... how did he mess that up? You're the one who killed her."

Everything around her felt so far away. Like her

head had been wrapped in cotton candy and muffled the sounds and smells and images.

Stay awake, girl. You have to stay awake.

Mason roared with anger. "You can't tell me you don't know! Jack must tell you everything—you two are thick as thieves! In case you didn't realize it, he's obsessed with you."

She felt herself sliding sideways on the stones until her head rested on the dirt. At least she couldn't feel her shoulder anymore through the haze. "Jack and I just work together...."

"*He told her!*" Mason bellowed so loudly his words reverberated off the stones.

"Told her what?" Rylie practically whispered.

"About my past! How could he tell her that?" he wailed. "The way she looked at me after finding out what happened to that kid? It was awful. I couldn't let her think that way about me."

Flicking the lighter once more, he held it in front of his face, morphing his features into a demon's image.

"So, you proved her right by killing my friend in your own fit of rage."

"A man has to do what a man has to do sometimes." He laughed again, the vitriol in his voice making her sick to her stomach.

She heard a loud slam that sent Mason out of sight and his lit lighter sailing down the wooden steps, straight for her. The second it made contact with the moisture on the stairs, flames burst free.

"No!" Rylie yelled as the entire world around her went black.

CHAPTER TWENTY

CARTER REACHED THE EDGE OF THE SMALL clearing where the stone shanty stood. The scent of gasoline filled the air. That could only mean one thing—someone planned to set a big fire. Kind of like the size of a cabin on a campground.

Someone stood in the entryway of the structure. Thanks to a full moon in a clear sky overhead, he could see the man very clearly.

"Mason?" Rylie's voice sounded from inside the building.

Who the heck was Mason?

A few seconds later, the man referred to Jack as his twin brother. Holy hell, this was the man who killed Rylie's boss! He'd avoided all mention of the incident in the media for months, wanting the man who had changed his entire life to remain faceless. Yet, here he stood, in person. Aside from longer hair and a rougher appearance, the man looked exactly like his brother. Which made absolute sense, given that Carter now knew they were twins.

The man Jay thought was Jack was actually his twin.

So, where was Jack?

All the evidence had pointed straight to the cameraman, but as Carter stood there in the shadows, listening, Mason admitted to every single crime.

Mason—Jack's twin—had set his own brother up for murder. He'd framed him as a serial killer. And now it looked like Rylie would be his next victim.

Like hell she would.

Carter grabbed a large rock off the ground and ran toward Mason, who had his back to him. When he got close enough to take the shot, he slammed it onto the killer's head. Mason flew forward, dropping the lighter and igniting the gasoline on the wooden steps.

"Rylie!" he yelled, catching sight of her in the light of the flames several feet from the steps.

Carter plunged forward, running down the rickety wood structure and hugging the wall to avoid the fire. All he could think about was getting to Rylie.

He had to save her. No way could he let another person die at that maniac's hand.

Halfway down the steps, a loud crack sounded. Sparks flew up in the air all around him, landing on his hair and his clothes, but Carter barely noticed. He was too busy crashing to the dirt floor as the entire staircase collapsed in a burst of flames that was followed by darkness.

Carter came to, hearing someone yelling his name. By some miracle, when the steps gave way, he'd rolled away from the pile of burning wood. The smoke was thick, and his right arm hurt badly. The smell of burning flesh made him want to vomit, but he ignored the pain and the churning in his stomach as he searched for Rylie. She hadn't moved since he first saw her, but the fire had drawn closer thanks to the pile of burning wood that had been their only way out.

"Marshall! Wake up, man! You okay?" The worried voice of his nemesis Detective Peters called down to him.

"Peters! That you?" Carter tested his limbs, and they all seemed to be functional, if in pain.

"I don't know how you got here when you're supposed to be on lockdown, but we're gonna get you both out of there! Can you walk?"

"Yeah, I'm pretty sure." Carter pulled himself to his feet with the help of the wall. The smoke had gotten pretty thick, making him cough. He pulled the neckline of his hoodie up over his nose. "I gotta get to Rylie! The fire is almost reaching her!"

"If you can get her out of the way, we'll find a way to pull you both out!"

Peters yelled a few commands to the officers with him that Carter couldn't quite make out. His focus was only on saving Rylie.

Using the wall for support, he stayed close to the moss-covered stones. The heat became intense as he got closer to where she lay. His injured arm had gone oddly numb, indicating his burn was probably pretty bad.

He'd worry about that later.

By the time he got to Rylie, the flames had spread to within inches of her feet. Using his good arm, he grabbed her by the waist of her jeans and tugged as hard as he could, dragging her to the far side of the room, where the temperature dropped about fifty degrees. Settling into the darkest, dampest corner, he pulled her close, cradling her head against his chest.

"Hang in there, Rylie. You're gonna be just fine." He whispered the same phrase over and over again, trying to convince himself it was true as his own vision began to darken and the fire and smoke faded away completely.

***

"MARSHALL! COME ON, MAN—WAKE UP."

Carter slowly came out of the darkness to see Peters hovering over him, shining a flashlight in his face.

"Dude, lose the light, would ya?" He tried to reach up and push the flashlight away, but his arm felt like lead.

The light shifted away from his face. "Don't try to move. The bird is coming in to take you to Trauma." He turned to another cop. "Maybe you can talk some sense into his stubborn skull."

Carter tried to sit up, but someone held his shoulders. "Would you just lie still, Carter. You don't want to make things worse."

Josh hovered over him, looking worried.

"What's going on, Josh?" Carter searched his brother's face for an answer. "Where's Rylie?"

"They got her out, too, but she's still unconscious. We called for LifeFlight to come and get you both."

Again, he tried to sit up, but Josh held him down.

"You've got some burns on your head and face. Your arm's a hot mess, though, brother. Your shooting arm. The less you move right now, the better."

Josh looked like he might cry. Josh never cried. Or showed much emotion at all.

His shooting arm. The gravity of that statement sank in like the rock he'd used to smack the killer.

Before he could ask if they got Mason in custody, a massive light flooded the area. The LifeFlight helicopter.

It was a slow, tedious process, putting first Rylie into the rescue basket and lifting her to the bird, then him. In the helicopter, they lay side by side. With his good hand, he reached over and grasped hers, fading in and out of consciousness as the helo carried them to the closest trauma center.

"Don't be dead, Rylie," he whispered. "I think I might be in love with you."

He couldn't be sure if it was real or he just wanted it to be, but he could have sworn she squeezed his hand and said, "I love you too," as he faded out of consciousness.

EPILOGUE

Nine Months Later

"NEED ANY HELP, BROTHER?"

Josh stood on the other side of the pile of wood Carter was trying to stack. Since the skin graft surgery for his third-degree burn, his right arm and hand stayed so tight. A simple task like stacking wood, something he would have knocked out in no time before the fire, now took him three times as long.

He sighed, tossing a log onto the pile. "Physical therapy isn't working, Josh. I don't think I'll ever have full function again."

His days were now spent in PT, taking pain

meds, and hoping he'd have enough dexterity to button his own jeans when he left the bathroom.

Josh clapped him lightly on the shoulder. "Give it time, Carter. You had a lot of damage."

He picked up another log with his left hand and added it to the stack. "I know. I just think it's time I face facts. This campground is all I have now. And I'm honestly okay with that. I just need to be able to take care of it. And this arm of mine is making it really hard right now."

He hadn't spoken to Rylie since the night of the fire. Last he'd heard, she'd gone home to LA to recover at her parents' home.

Giving up on the woodpile, he shoved his hands into the pockets of his jacket. "I think I'm gonna take a walk, Josh. Lock up the office when you leave, okay?"

"Want me to tag along? Maybe we could drop a line in the water?" Josh looked at him, a hint of worry in his eyes.

Carter shook his head. "No, thanks. I want to be alone."

"I get it." Josh seemed hesitant to let him go. "Give me a call later, though, okay?"

"I will." He started to walk away but stopped and turned back around. "Have you heard from Jay?

I know he was really upset when I was in the hospital."

Josh nodded. "After he gave his statement to the police and Mason was sent back to maximum security, his old man went on a bender and ended up locked up for a hit-and-run. His aunt on his mother's side came and took him home with her. Last text I got, he sent a picture of himself standing on the beach in the Outer Banks in a wet suit with a surfboard. He looked real good, Carter."

Carter smiled. "That's the best thing I've heard in months."

Josh returned the smile. "You did good by him, Carter. Letting him work off his debt for the vandalism gave him a new perspective on life. He has a chance now at more than a future in lockup like his old man. Maybe you ought to give him a call sometime. I know he'd like to hear from you."

That had to be the most his baby brother had ever said at one time. Everyone seemed to be going through some major changes.

Everyone except for him. At least, not positive ones. His changes had made him more alone.

"Yeah, maybe. Someday." Carter walked toward the path to his favorite place, the waterfall.

For late February, the sun felt nice and warm.

Carter worked up a sweat hiking to the falls. Of course, his body was a lot less strong than it used to be, but six weeks in the burn unit followed by a couple major surgeries would do that to a guy.

Settling on the bank, Carter stretched out and lay back on the cold ground. The only thing he ever felt anymore was the cold. It reminded him that he could still feel *something* even if his emotions had decided to go on hiatus.

As he lay there, a flock of birds suddenly startled, taking to the skies from the trees behind him.

"Is this spot taken?"

Carter shot up to a seated position and turned to look toward the trees. Rylie stood there, smiling at him.

The urge to run and hide his hideous self slammed full force into the urge to take her in his deformed arms and kiss her until the sun rose the next morning.

Instead of doing either of those things, he pulled his sleeves down and shoved his hands into his pants pockets, trying to hide the things he hated to look at.

"No one's sitting there. I'll leave and give you some peace." He couldn't bring himself to make eye contact. The burn scars on his face were still pretty red. She didn't need to see that.

Rylie sat down beside him, placing her hand on his knee. "I don't want to be alone. I came here to see you."

"Why would you do that?" *Great, Carter, now you sound like a real jerk.*

She turned her body so she faced him. "You wouldn't return my calls or emails, so I decided to come see for myself that you're okay."

He looked away from her. "I'm fine."

Rylie reached up and placed her fingers on his cheek, slowing turning his head to face her. Carter flinched when her fingertips grazed one of his scars. "I also needed to say thank you in person."

He kept his gaze averted, still unable to make himself look at her. "For what?"

"You came for me. If it weren't for you, I wouldn't be here right now." She reached over and pulled his hand from his pocket, entwining her fingers with his. He tried to resist, but she wouldn't let him. "I've missed you."

He pulled his hand from hers and stood up, turning his back to her. "I'm glad you survived, and it looks like you've healed. You know, they put Mason back in maximum security, and he isn't allowed to do anything without a guard, so he can't ever escape again. They're even bringing his meals to him in his solitary cell. You'll be safe now." The words tumbled from him in a huge jumble.

He heard her stand up and walk over to where he stood. She wrapped her arms around his chest and hugged him from behind. He wanted to step away but couldn't make himself do it. Her touch felt so right. "That's good. Jack's still struggling knowing his brother is a serial killer. He feels guilty as hell that it was his twin killing those people to get back at him. You know where he was that day, don't you?"

Carter shook his head. "No one ever said."

"He got a message for a family emergency. Turns out it was Mason setting him up to be gone all day to make him look even more guilty."

"Why didn't the DOC alert Jack and his family that Mason had escaped?" That had bothered Carter for a long time.

She shrugged. "Somehow, it never got to Jack. A breakdown in communication somewhere. He could never get any answers on that."

"What about your show? I heard it was a huge hit. Are you making a second season?"

Rylie shook her head and let out a little laugh. "I think one was enough, don't you?"

"I suppose it was. So, did you and Jack finally get

together?" Carter asked quietly. "He's been in love with you forever, you know."

Rylie laughed as she walked around to stand in front of him. "You cannot be that thickskulled, can you, Carter Marshall?"

"What exactly do you mean?"

"You're a darn fool if you think Jack's the one I love." She moved in close and rose up on tiptoe, balancing herself with a hand resting on the back of his neck. "Why do I always have to be the one to kiss you?" She pressed her lips to his in the softest kiss he'd ever experienced.

"I'm not good for you," he whispered against her lips. "I'm not the man I used to be."

"That man said he wasn't right for me too." She kissed him again. "When are you going to stop telling me what I want, need, and feel? I love you, silly man. And I know you love me too."

He frowned. "How?"

She smiled and kissed him a third time. "Because you told me."

In the helicopter. She'd heard him. All these months, he'd convinced himself she hadn't—that she'd been unconscious. That meant he'd really heard her say it too. His heart skipped a beat in his chest with the happiness flooding through him.

Then he remembered.

Stepping back to put some distance between them, he shook his head. "Rylie, everything is different now." He pulled the sleeve up on his right arm, exposing the rough, discolored skin there. "My arm isn't getting back to where it should be. I'll probably never be whole again."

Closing the distance between them, she gently placed her hand on his scarred arm. "Last I heard, you were going to make this place a survival training destination. Pretty amazing thing for people to be trained by a real live survival expert and all. Remember?"

"Yeah, well, I wasn't broken then."

She lifted her hand and pressed her palm to his cheek. "You saved me, Carter. And you got justice for Darcy. A few scars don't make you broken or any less of a man. They're a testament to the amazingly strong, brave hero I am so completely in love with that I quit my job and moved back to Staunton to remind you that you are also in love with me too."

He searched her eyes for any indication she wasn't telling the truth, but all he saw there was love.

"You really did that, didn't you?" he asked.

She smiled and nodded. "I did. And no matter how long it takes me, I'm going to prove to you that you're worthy of happiness and love. I don't care about your scarred arm, and I'm actually pretty glad you're not a cop. I don't want to worry about you every day. I want to hang out here, on our mountain, and live out our days in peace and quiet—together."

Our mountain. For the first time in forever, Carter actually felt something other than sadness and guilt. Joy and peace and love took turns assaulting him. The images of him and Rylie spending the rest of their days together filled his mind and gave him such a rush of emotion, he wrapped his arms around her and kissed her like he'd never kissed anyone before.

As his lips met hers, he offered up a promise of love, friendship, and a future. Holding her close, his injured arm worked just fine, as though that were the only job it wanted for the rest of his life.

"Thank you," he said, resting his forehead against hers.

"For what?" She ran her fingers though the hair at the base of his neck.

"For coming back." He kissed her again, suddenly unable to get enough of her. "I love you, Rylie. I may not be very good at it right now, but I promise to spend every single day getting better at it."

"I love you too. But you know that already. Because you heard me that night also." She leaned her head against his chest. "I'd say the universe has spoken."

"And who are we to question the universe?" He wrapped an arm around her shoulders and started walking them back to the cabins. "Come on, let me show you around our mountain. We can check out the view from my cabin."

He leaned down and kissed her once more. Suddenly the future seemed bright and full of hope, love, and happiness—and for once in a very long time, Carter thought maybe he was okay with that.

ACKNOWLEDGMENTS

This book has been a true labor of love. With every possible obstacle standing in the way, I finally got it all on the page. Thank you so much to McKinley for understanding my brain and pointing the way to making this book the absolute best it can be. I have only worked with one other editor who could do that, and I am blessed to have found it again. Thank you also to Kristin for cleaning up the things I struggle with most—those darn commas! Thank you to Becky and all the staff of Hot Tree for putting my book babies out there with so much passion. I am thrilled and grateful to work with such an amazing team.

Thank you to my ever-supportive husband, who makes up a tiny part of every hero I create. Your self-less service to others for so many years has provided so many opportunities for me to celebrate you in my books. Every woman should have a real live hero in her life. I'm so fortunate to have you as mine.

Finally, to Carlos—I hope you love your character! I used all my favorites of your qualities, from your incredibly likable personality to your creative stories and talent for working with people. Thank you for the inspiration!

ABOUT THE AUTHOR

Carolyn LaRoche is a retired high school teacher. She lives in southeast Virginia with her husband, a retired police officer, and their two sons. Her four cats and rescue pup serve as supervisors to her writing that began over twenty-five years ago. With nearly twenty books and short stories to her credit, Carolyn applies her degree in forensic science and her love of all things suspense and mystery to each of her stories. Who doesn't love a little romance amid a shootout or fiery crash?

Join Carolyn's newsletter:

WWW.CAROLYNLAROCHE.WORDPRESS.COM

Carolyn would love to hear from you directly too. Please feel free to email her at CAROLYNLAROCHEAU THOR@YAHOO.COM or check out her website WWW.CAROLYNLAROCHE.WORDPRESS.COM for updates.

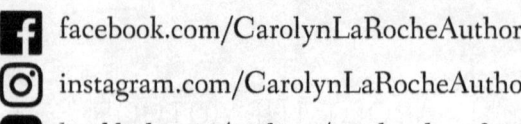

facebook.com/CarolynLaRocheAuthor

instagram.com/CarolynLaRocheAuthor

bookbub.com/authors/carolyn-laroche

ABOUT THE PUBLISHER

Hot Tree Publishing loves love. Publishing adult romantic fiction, HTPubs are all about diverse reads featuring heroes and heroines to swoon over. Since opening in 2015, HTPubs have published more than 350 titles across the wide and diverse range of romantic genres. If you're chasing a happily ever after in your favourite subgenre, HTPubs have you covered.

Interested in discovering more amazing reads brought to you by Hot Tree Publishing? Head over to the website for information:

WWW.HOTTREEPUBLISHING.COM

facebook.com/hottreepublishing
instagram.com/hottreepublishing
tiktok.com/@hottreepublishing